SOBERBI
I0769445

THE LEGACY SERIES

Series Titles

Salt Folk
Ryan Habermeyer

The Machine We Trust
Tim Conrad

Gridlock
Brett Biebel

The Commission of Inquiry
Patrick Nevins

Maximum Speed
Kevin Clouther

Reach Her in This Light
Jane Curtis

The Spirit in My Shoes
John Michael Cummings

*The Effects of Urban Renewal on Mid-Century America and
Other Crime Stories*
Jeff Esterholm

What Makes You Think You're Supposed to Feel Better
Jody Hobbs Hesler

Fugitive Daydreams
Leah McCormack

Hoist House: A Novella & Stories
Jenny Robertson

Finding the Bones: Stories & A Novella
Nikki Kallio

Praise for

SALT FOLK

"Reading Ryan Habermeyer's stories is like being given a tour of an eccentric inventor's laboratory. There's a lovely whir all around you, delicate ratchets and clicks. Dozens of clockwork devices crank through unknowable tasks. And no matter how closely you watch, from the flick of a switch to the final electrical zap, you never follow exactly how you find, in your open palms, each story's small miracle."

—Zach Powers
author of *Gravity Changes*

"The Utah in Ryan Habermeyer's *Salt Folk* is more wondrous and surreal than even its otherworldly landscapes. It's also, as Habermeyer writes in one story, 'a cruel place. The weird orphan of the West nobody invites to the birthday party.' In the relentlessly inventive stories of this standout collection, one character jump humps mannequins, another cleans up the mess of other people's spilt emotions, and still another spends her days masturbating the last elephant on Earth. Habermeyer is a fearless and ardent writer. His sentences shimmer, startle, and slay. I urge you to read this book."

—Michelle Ross
author of *They Kept Running*

"This salty, unfiltered collection will immerse you in sensation, from marvel to horror, sorrow to lust. Habermeyer, an extraordinary stylist, polishes each sentence until we can see eternity in its grain. Along the way, he introduces us to a world of marvels—glaciers and jellyfish, elephants and yeti, angels and ghosts—all transformed through the alchemy of his prose."

—Trudy Lewis
author of *The Empire Rolls*

"The crazed crystalline stories found in Ryan Habermeyer's multifaceted *Salt Folk* work together like cantilevered mobiles of pristine prisms chiming in a gale force wind of pure segmented light—laminations of litanies, collaged matrices, sonic booms and tectonic tangos. Habermeyer is a master mason of the 'Worry,' a flat deadpan form that deepens after each clear-coated application of lacquered language and steel-wooled sanded syntax. The result: textured texts of high-gloss depths that suggest and then, suddenly, deliver ecstatic endlessnesses and infinitely mirrored infinites."

—Michael Martone
author of *Plain Air: Sketches from Winesburg, Indiana*

"*Salt Folk*, the new collection of stories by Ryan Habermeyer, astounds as one of the most innovative and eclectic collections I've read in some time. Each story explodes with a wallop of a premise, followed by Habermeyer meeting his own bar with flawless execution of unforgettable characters, unforeseeable twists, and profound observation. I read all of these stories with wild abandon, speeding through the pages, only to find myself rewarded time and again. The worst moment in the book is when it ends, but hopefully, this is only a glimpse of what is to come from this talented and daring author."

—Michael Czyzniejewski
author of *The Amnesiac in the Maze*

Salt Folk

STORIES

Ryan Habermeyer

CORNERSTONE PRESS

UNIVERSITY OF WISCONSIN-STEVENS POINT

Cornerstone Press, Stevens Point, Wisconsin 54481
Copyright © 2024 Ryan Habermeyer
www.uwsp.edu/cornerstone

Printed in the United States of America by
Point Print and Design Studio, Stevens Point, Wisconsin

Library of Congress Control Number: 2024900349
ISBN: 978-1-960329-34-9

Cover art and frontispiece by Andrew Rice. Used by permission of the artist.

This is a work of fiction. Names, characters, businesses, places, events, and incidents
are either the products of the author's imagination or used in a fictitious manner. Any
resemblance to actual persons, living or dead, or actual events is purely coincidental.

Cornerstone Press titles are produced in courses and internships offered by the
Department of English at the University of Wisconsin–Stevens Point.

DIRECTOR & PUBLISHER
Dr. Ross K. Tangedal

EXECUTIVE EDITORS
Jeff Snowbarger, Freesia McKee

EDITORIAL DIRECTOR
Ellie Atkinson

SENIOR EDITORS
Brett Hill, Grace Dahl

PRESS STAFF
Madalyn Carpenter, Chloe Cieszynski, Carolyn Czerwinski, Alex Diaz, Sophie
McPherson, Josh Paulson, Natalie Reiter, Ava Willett

For Mother,
who birthed salt that lost its savor

Also by Ryan Habermeyer:

The Science of Lost Futures

CONTENTS

Author's Note

The photos in "A North American Field Guide to Glaciers" are reprinted courtesy of the Ralph Stockman Tarr collection, "Historic Glacial Images of Alaska and Greenland," at Cornell University Library (https://digital.library.cornell.edu/collections/tarr). "Teeth Like God's Shoeshine" derives its title from the eponymous song by Modest Mouse, and like many blues songs, "It Hurts Me Too," has been recorded and performed by multiple artists—the story "Go Wrong with You" contains lines from the Elmore James version, although I have lightly tweaked the lyrics. Finally, "Wife No. 57" was inspired by and composed after consulting the following historical texts: Edward W. Tullidge, *Life of Brigham Young: Or, Utah and Her Founders*; Susa Young Gates, *Brigham Young: Patriot, Pioneer, and Prophet*; Stanley P. Hirshson, *The Lion of the Lord: A Biography of Brigham Young*; Leonard J. Arrington, *Brigham Young: American Moses*; John G. Turner, *Brigham Young: Pioneer Prophet*; with a special thanks to Virginia Kerns's brilliant monograph, *Sally in Three Worlds: An Indian Captive in the House of Brigham Young*, without which my story would not exist. I trust readers to discover my historical liberties.

*"Come now," the king said, "speak again. How much
do you love me, my dear?" And the princess said,
"I love you like salt."*

—English folktale

*But his wife looked back from behind him,
and she became a pillar of salt.*

—Book of Genesis 19:26

*I shivered in those solitudes
when I heard the voice of
the salt in the desert*

—Pablo Neruda

La Petite Mort

Every morning, the elephant masturbator lures the elephant into the cage by humming Bach. The elephant, blind and tuskless, lumbers slowly onto the hay, kneeling like a prince, obviously in love with the low, languid melody.

———————

The elephant masturbator continues humming as she administers the sedative, stares into the elephant's wet, glossy eyes as it slips into wherever it is elephants go when they dream. She rubs his trunk. She counts: three, two, one.

———————

As the elephant masturbator gently arouses the elephant, she traces the wrinkles on its skin. Here is a scar from fleeing the poachers. Here is a reddish patch that may or may not be an infection. Here are the freckles she's named Larry, Curly, Moe.

———————

By the time the elephant awakens, the elephant masturbator has scavenged a meal of twigs, roots, leaves, and the last two yellow flower petals in this part of the world. Watching the elephant eat, the elephant masturbator tells the elephant about Hanno, the elephant of Pope Leo X. And Surus, who crossed the Alps with Hannibal. And a nameless pachyderm, knighted by Henry III, who died drinking too much red wine while consoling the grief-stricken king. Once home, the elephant masturbator pours herself a glass of sour wine and sits on her balcony, staring at the haze of neon lights and listening to sirens echo, wondering why she stays in this desert, in this city like the edge of a map torn off that nobody bothered to tape back together. She listens to Bach. She prefers the fugues in D minor. She drinks more wine.

———

At dawn, the elephant masturbator arouses the elephant after which they go for a walk.

———

At dusk, the elephant masturbator arouses the elephant after which they go for a walk.

———

At the restaurant, the elephant masturbator eats mealworms sautéed in a kind of yellow pesto with a side of fried crickets. The man sitting across from her talks about trying to save the last butterflies from extinction. He rubs his thumb on the white tablecloth until it leaves a greasy stain. The emaciated waitress fills their cups with brownish water. It's important work we're doing, he says. You have a cricket leg in your teeth, she says.

After her date, the elephant masturbator visits the elephant and pushes fruit rinds buzzing with flies through the cage bars. She rubs his trunk and tells him about the man with the combover. The elephant leans against the cage and sighs, like he wants to be touched.

Mwisho, she calls him, which in Swahili means *the end*.

The elephant masturbator sponges water over Mwisho's ears, legs, stomach. She's careful around his eyes. She knows how this will end. Alone, floating towards her petite mort, she imagines the shriveled elephant carcass carried away by devoted ants until there's just a keyboard of bones in the dust. It'd be nice, she thinks, if she was also a sacrament.

Most of the time when the elephant climaxes there's just a noise. *Poof.* Like air let out of a tire. On a good day, the elephant masturbator collects the sperm in a plastic container. It looks cloudy, like a root beer float.

The elephant masturbator bottles and seals the container. Scribbles descriptions on the label. Sometimes includes a note. *We're still here.* Ships them at the post office to the scientists she's not sure even exist. She sits on her porch steps and waits for mail that never comes.

———————

The elephant masturbator closes her eyes on the bed and thinks of Mwisho from the inside out. Organs to skeleton to skin. She feels oddly happy at the inexplicableness of it all.

———————

Leaving the restaurant, the combover man takes her hand as they walk through what was once the Great Salt Lake, dried up like a bowl licked clean by a greedy toddler. Kids with red scaly patches around their eyes scare away gulls from the debris. The arsenic haze steams yellow. The elephant masturbator's eyes sting, her nostrils burn. She wonders what people used to do for foreplay.

———————

The elephant masturbator powders Mwisho with dust. She shoos away flies. Steals pillows from the abandoned hotels and spreads them on the cage floor. Removes lice. Pedicures debris between his toes. Brushes teeth. Then it's time to start over and powder him with dust.

———————

The elephant masturbator keeps coins in her pocket. As they walk, the coins make a metallic swish. The elephant likes to filch the coins with his trunk. Sometimes the elephant masturbator will do a magic trick her mother taught her and make a coin disappear then reappear behind the elephant's floppy ear. The elephant smiles but does not laugh.

The elephant masturbator sponges the elephant and rubs away dead skin, counting the moles on the elephant's flank. Larry, Curly, Moe. She's been trying to get the elephant to laugh. The chimps are gone. Foxes, dolphins, cows—all gone. All the laughing things extinct. Even the butterflies, which never laughed, are almost gone, says the combover man at the restaurant trying to save them. She pulls faces for the elephant, falls off the stool, tries to get him to mimic her: *nyuk nyuk nyuk*.

The elephant masturbator saves a butterfly caught in a spider's web on the windowsill. Its wing is broken. She squishes it between her fingers, its juices stickying her skin for days.

They walk and walk and walk. Out of nowhere the desert opens into a canyon. The elephant masturbator leans over the edge. Who knows how long it has been there, this earthy mouth like the scar of some geological castration.

____

The elephant masturbator doesn't tell Mwisho her name. She doesn't tell Mwisho about her scars. She doesn't tell him about the things that make her laugh. She doesn't tell him how in the old war the Germans dropped elephants out of planes when they ran out of bombs. She doesn't tell Mwisho how after her father died in Afghanistan she started sleeping on the stairs, anxious to twist herself into something else, disappointed that she is still flesh and bone.

____

Mwisho scuffs his foot in the dirt. The elephant masturbator stomps her foot in response, knowing Mwisho will not call her *unlucky* or *needy* or *unlovable*.

____

There are so many kinds of laughter, the elephant masturbator tells Mwisho as she traces a finger over Larry, Curly, and Moe. Funny laugh. Mean laugh. Sad laugh. Nervous laugh. Sick laugh. Laughing to keep from crying. Laughing to forget. Dying laughter. Laughing to remember. Which kind of laughter do you want to be?

____

The elephant masturbator's hands do not shake as she steadies the syringe and empties the sedative into the elephant. But they always tremble when she reaches for the glass of wine at the restaurant. It's just nerves, she smiles. I promise not to bite, the man smiles. She stares out the window at the desert. Hidden beneath the dust she imagines the skeletons of creeping things fossilized in radioactive prayer.

———

Sometimes the sedative frightens the elephant. It gives him bad dreams. He twitches until the cage feels like it might collapse. He must be coaxed into romance. At first, she had to reach her arm up his rectum, elbow-deep, and finger a golf-ball-sized gland until the long gray shaft emerged. But now she knows Mwisho prefers she rubs his foot. Elephants speak through their feet, talking and listening through vibrations. So, she rubs his foot that doubles as a tongue and ear, surprised to discover Mwisho has no interest in sex. He wants a lover. He wants words.

———

Still, it's a precarious moment. She's been careless before. One wrong touch and the jumbo organ whips back and forth like an errant fire hose, slapping her right below the eye. Sperm bubbles in the dirt. Fool, she tells herself, her ears still ringing hours later. She waits for the wound to bleed but it never does. At night she looks in the mirror as the skin welts and swells and the bruise goes from purple to yellow to gray. She tries to collect other bruises to show the elephant, to hold her skin up to its blind eyes to say, See?

———

You speak of this elephant as a lover, the man smiles. Her insides knot hearing love spoken of with such quiet malice.

Love is a strong word, she says, playing with her fork. The moon doesn't exist for the tide, the man tells her. What tides? she wants to say.

———

The elephant masturbator yawns. The elephant yawns too.

———

We're lucky, the elephant masturbator says, stroking Mwisho. Some survive and some vanish and some never exist at all.

———

There's nobody left at the zoo. Nobody who knows she's here all day, masturbating an elephant, last of his kind. You have nice hands, her mother told her when she was a girl. When she saw the graffiti downtown, *laugh of a lifesick elephant* in neon letters, she went to the zoo thinking this was the nicest thing to do with her hands. There was no advertisement. No application, no interview. No training, no internship, no exams on the history and scholarship surrounding pachyderm arousal methods. But somebody did it before her. For decades, it seems. All the equipment is here. The illustrated notebooks, the vials, the syringes, the lotions, the aprons, the goggles, the electro-ejaculators. But the elephant masturbator uses none of these. Just one skin to another. And Bach. Always Bach.

The elephant masturbator bathes Mwisho. His favorite is when she lathers him in mud, but it's getting harder and harder to find water these days. The lakes have dried up. Rivers too. Most nights the elephant masturbator can hear the neighbors singing hymns in the chapel. A graveyard of prayers.

Have you always been a pixie? the man asks, spooning gray paste into his mouth. She runs fingers through her hair nervously. Not always, she says. You're very mysterious, the man says later, tracing a finger over her wrinkled navel. I'm nobody, the elephant masturbator says, just a girl from Panguitch.

The elephant masturbator is tired of all this desert. Sand in your hair, your ears, under your nails, little grains stuck between your teeth. It's like for centuries people whacked off God until there was nothing left of him and now everyone is just waiting in his hot mute dust.

This isn't living, the elephant masturbator thinks. But it's not dying either.

———

Lately, when the elephant masturbator hums Bach Mwisho pretends to hide. His blind eyes forlorn. As if he knows something is being stolen from him.

———

Lately, Mwisho stares into the bucket as if wishing he was no longer blind and could see his reflection. She wonders if blindness is something light or heavy. She wonders if Mwisho is happy or sad to be blind. She wonders if she keeps giving away her happiness will it boomerang back eventually like a slap in the face?

———

Mwisho sprays her with his trunk. He smiles but does not laugh.

———

She spends an afternoon collecting and boiling rapeseed, skimming off the oil then grinding the pulp with a mortar and pestle into a rancid lubricant she spreads over Mwisho. He moans. Her hands are chafed and blistered. She can barely hold the pen to write letters to the scientists. Some nights when she can't sleep, she'll sneak into the factory and scavenge paraffin off the humming machines spitting out yellow plumes that bloat the sky. But looking into Mwisho's glazed eyes, she knows he prefers the rapeseed lube to the machinery grease. They wander the enclosures together, the elephant foraging here and there or playfully swatting her with his trunk. The grass used to be so green, she apologizes.

————————

The elephant masturbator knows she can give up whenever she wants. Nothing is keeping her here masturbating this elephant day after day after day. She is not waiting for a *thank you*. She is not looking for anything to fill the void of existence now that the curtain is falling on this thing called ecology. She does not believe this will change the course of the universe. She has no babies of her own and wants only to stare into the elephant's wet, blind eyes for reasons she doesn't want to understand.

————————

Later, there is just a puff of air. The elephant masturbator sighs.

————————

In the man's apartment, the elephant masturbator listens to the man play the piano. The ivory keys are brightly polished. Do you like Bach? Yes, the elephant masturbator says. Later, as his tongue traces the constellation of moles and scars on her stomach, she wonders if he is thinking about cunnilingus on a butterfly and whether he knows she is thinking about masturbating the elephant.

————————

Mwisho is easy, she tells herself. Bach. Bath. Syringe. Bach. Men are simple too, but also not simple.

———

The elephant yawns. The elephant masturbator yawns too.

———

The elephant masturbator stands in the desert at dusk. She wants to be a moon, but she knows she is the water waiting for the tide.

———

The man knocks on the elephant masturbator's door. She doesn't answer. She presses against the door and listens. She waits for him to knock again, waits to decode the vibrations of his desire. And her own.

———

The elephant masturbator grinds her foot in the dust. She stomps. Mwisho stomps his feet in the dust. There was a time when the elephant masturbator believed he was calling out to a lover, but she knows he knows he's the last of his kind. The elephant masturbator knows he's calling out to his mother, the keeper of elephant lore, asking her for the generational wisdom that vanished with the poacher's bullet. The elephant masturbator feels the ground tremble. The tickling crawls down her spine until it feels like a little death. The vibrations neither bitter nor melancholic. Strangely joyful. Part of her wants to believe he's trying to teach her his language. Beyond the snorts, grunts, roars, and cries. Beyond those low, dull rumbles the human ear cannot hear. The grinding, scuffing vibrations of the elephant foot. The foot that doubles as tongue and ear.

A North American
Field Guide to Glaciers

In November I returned to Salt Lake City after thirty-four years and while lost on one of those streets with no name ran into a childhood friend I almost didn't recognize because we'd both grown fat and wrinkled like widows in a Renaissance painting, and after an hour of idle chit-chat we retired to a hotel lobby where my friend shared the news that Yelena Zubredevya, the singularly odd Sunday school chorister, had walked out onto the glacier the night before and not returned, one week after her eighty-first birthday. I refused to believe it. Even after reviewing the breadcrumbs of her

life in the newspaper obituary, and even after my friend leaned close and confessed all these years she still heard Miss Z's voice in her ear, a voice which the doctor dismissed as mere tinnitus, and didn't I still hear voices too?—even then I doubted it was possible for Miss Z to be gone, for the presence of the glacier was proof that nothing was ever truly gone anymore, only displaced, like moving from one room to the next, and the more I tried to forget her the more my head began to swim with thoughts of Miss Z.

She lived on M street in the Avenues, no. 116, a house Brigham Young built for his favorite wife who went mad a century earlier. Miss Z was not religious, but she liked to tell people this inconsequential detail as she believed it lent her an aura of mystique and endeared her to the local Mormons who found her eccentric. Yelly Nellie, they used to call her. As a kid she was quite the talker. By the time we knew her the once flamboyant Queen Anne home was falling apart: the wood rotted, the roof a parliament for fungus, the windows soap scummed, and the yard a refuge for monstrous blooms of peppermint which Miss Z boiled and baked into candies. All the neighborhood children took piano lessons from her. The sticky fingers and icy peppermint throat were the hard-earned reward for enduring half

an hour under her strict tutelage as she disciplined our fingers to know a note after a note after a note could form something that was greater and more meaningful than the individual sounds. I could still picture her smile. Her teeth were weirdly white. Like God's shoeshine, she used to say.

Her methods were unconventional. God may speak English, she used to say, but music knows only Italian. Before touching the piano, she required a rudimentary knowledge of the language. For a time, the playground was abuzz with phrases like *Sputa il rospo!* and *In bocca al lupo!* She took all her pupils—even the frightened ones like me—to the Utah State asylum to converse with an elderly Italian gentleman who talked for more than an hour about his native homeland, by that time submerged in the Mediterranean by rising sea levels. Wild stories, no doubt, based on his facial expressions, but completely incomprehensible, and it all must have been too much for him because one afternoon  Miss Z said he'd drowned himself in the bathtub. She never raised her voice above a whisper, sitting on the piano bench with eyes closed, mildly catatonic, tapping the beat with her fingers, moving slowly and with great difficulty because of one withered leg covered in milky scars, the result of a childhood illness or accident we never knew. Halfway through a lesson her eyes would suddenly fling open and she would dole out peppermints and regale us with stories of composers. Hildegard von Bingen who wore a girdle of thorns to summon angelic choirs. Mozart who penned lullabies to his cousin about shitting on her face. Clara Schumann whose talents far surpassed those of her more famous husband. And our favorite, poor Haydn's head, decapitated and robbed from his grave and kept in the bed of a Viennese opera singer who hoped to divine its musical genius.

Even though I enjoyed these macabre stories more than playing the piano itself I knew they were prelude to a trip to the glacier at the end of each lesson where we stood at the icefront listening to the groans and gasps of deforming ice, a soundtrack that left me with the anxiety that to exist in this world things must be either very large or very small and anything in between would surely disappear. Miss Z encouraged me to get uncomfortably close to it, put my hands on it even, something my superstitious parents warned me never to do. They had heard rumors. How early in the epidemic at a recital in Miss Z's house a student, a snot-faced boy who teased everyone at school, suddenly crumpled into ice mid-performance. Miss Z, supposedly, walked slowly from the back of the room. She swept up what was left of the ice boy into a bucket and finished his performance—Chopin's Impromptu No. 66, I think—without batting an eye. She was the only one in the valley we knew whose body was untouched by glacier. Not even a little ice patch like the rest of us eventually had on our knees and elbows. As if the

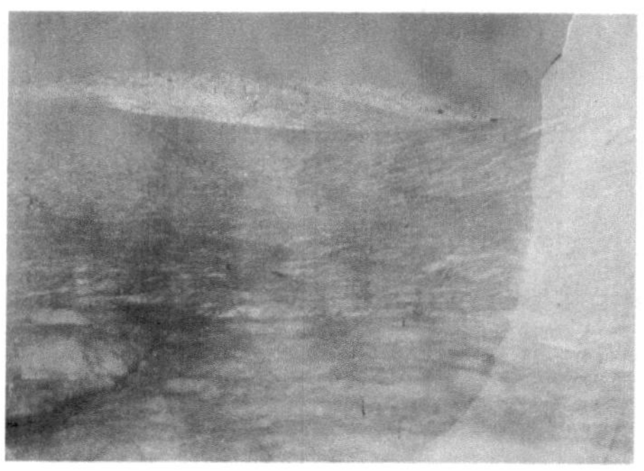

glacier was afraid of, maybe even mesmerized by, her.

I never asked if the rumors were true. When the sky grew dark, she walked me home in silence.

I remained at the deserted hotel as long as I could. Spying the glacier from a distance it was obvious that after enduring the sun all day it preferred the moon, soaking up its glow as if they were lovers. Too anxious to visit my childhood neighborhood, I wandered the streets aimlessly, finding empty doorways and abandoned bicycles, the echoes of *cane baby, cane baby, cane baby*, still rattling around my head, that old nickname of mine because I was never without one of Miss Z's candy canes hanging from my lip, then crossing the railroad tracks past the slaughterhouse and glassworks and fabric

warehouses, all strangely silent, only the fertilizer plant coughing yellow smoke from its chimneys, suddenly overcome with a longing for nightfall until remembering night hardly existed here anymore owing to the glacier whose soft whiteness illuminated the desert and inspired a city of insomniacs of whom I was the most recent convert.

As I walked, I recalled the early days of the glacier, its slow advancement from uneven patches of ice confusing scientists until becoming a fat white tongue thickening in the dried-out lakebed, and how for so long we had resigned ourselves to the emptiness that comes with extinction, no longer hopeful of rewilding, no longer sunbeams in Sunday school singing praises but chanting under our breaths *Jesus wants me for a catastrophe*, that we surrendered to the glacier's demands willingly and without question. If Miss

Z had indeed walked out into the glacier it was nothing exceptional. Every day of my childhood men and women wandered silently into its emptiness. And the glacier grew whiter and thicker.

When, in the nature of things, there were no more children for piano lessons, Miss Z opened a kiosk near Stansbury Bay, the eastern edge of the glacier that was often slightly pinkish from algae blooms, where she sold bouquets of bright plastic flowers. Sometimes a feral cat wandered by, ignoring her efforts to entice it with peppermint candies. Otherwise, she was alone. Little by little her reputation was almost equal to that of the glacier. Many despised her and found her diligent caretaking, what they called her affection, unnatural. Others loved her and made it a point to visit her kiosk. As is the nature of things, her strangeness was soon ignored and forgotten. In the evenings she chiseled away a bucket of glacier ice for boiling confectionary sugar water and could be seen limping up the steep hill back home. Nobody offered to help.

It had been years since I'd seen the glacier up close. It was far bigger than I remembered: a vast, monstrous whiteness.

My mind balked at the size of it, distressed how the earth could imagine something so alien. Most people seeing the glacier up close for the first time are stunned. Utah is so far west, so unreal, it feels like an alien planet. And the desert. So much desert. If visitors remember history lessons from middle school, it's only antique photos of the old Salt Lake with pioneers floating like pickles. Of course, they remember the news bulletins of the megadrought and vanishing lake, reporters covered in arsenic dust with the unapologetic sun leaving an empty dustbowl in the background. But people now have a hard time looking at the glacier with its weird unnerving beauty. Like it doesn't belong here. Like it isn't really a glacier because a glacier must have a hidden flow and move beneath the weight of its own unbearable mass, becoming what one polar explorer called a *faint dreamy color music, a faraway, long-drawn-out melody on muted strings.* And yet it's always there, the glacier, whether you believed it or not, just there, a savage ominous thereness.

I kept my distance, perched on the nearby rocks like a gull, waiting for someone to tell me what I came for.

The kiosk was disheveled. As if Miss Z expected to return. I tried to picture her on the wobbly stool, mildly catatonic as the halogen bulb attracted moths and her gnarled and callused fingers glued together plastic flowers. I tried to imagine her walking out into that strange whiteness, her body dwarfed until slowly dissolving like a grain of sugar on a tongue. Most women her age had at least a few visible icy patches, their wrinkles scarred over from tiny seizures of joy that crystalized and chafed the skin, but I imagined she was soft and smooth, her body slender like an eel. I rummaged boxes, hoping I'd find some memento of her, perhaps even the sculpture I'd made, a glass Chopin death mask, the only gift I'd ever given anyone, assembled from jagged bits and pieces stolen from the glassworks and windows shattered around town. I left it on her doorstep on the anniversary of the composer's birthday thinking at my next lesson she would put it on display near the piano, but I never saw it again, and in shame I had stumbled over the notes so badly she put her hands over mine, my face flushed wild red. It was the one time I felt she'd thought of me as more alive than the glacier. She would sometimes spend entire lessons telling me about the crystalline structure of ice, millions of microscopic crystals stacked on top of each other, pressing and sighing in a sea of frozen lattices, the ice layering on ice exponentially, like skin, and even if she believed she could escape it, which she did not, she knew she could never escape it, that even brief day trips away from the city upset her and that the glacier had left an invisible mark on her. It had, I remember her saying, *taken possession of her*, crowding out her memories until there was nothing of her left.

I thumbed through an old photograph bin. As best I could tell, Miss Z had been taking pictures off and on for years using an old tripod camera that was collecting dust in the corner, developing the negatives in a closet or bathtub with harsh chemicals that probably turned her hair white, slowly, because everything is slow now. Some were of the crumbling downtown shops in her hometown of Goshen. Most were blurry, the images grainy and warped with double exposure, but the glacier always loomed like a cabaret dancer. Her photographic obsession started as a kind of romance, I told myself, like she was trying to capture a lover unaware, but a lover that disgusted her, only to find herself surrendering to the fascination of disgust. I was glad I wasn't here to see her like this. It is a difficult thing to watch someone love something that doesn't love them back. Eventually, she turned the photos into postcards which she mailed indiscriminately all over the world with the same cryptic message scribbled on the back: *Dillo al ghiaccio*. Go tell it to the ice.

One of the postcards ended up in the hands of some Czech tourists in whose company I found myself after circling the streets until sunrise. They'd come for the glacier. But whether to witness it or become part of it I couldn't tell. We made loops around the city. Wandering up the canyon before surveying Temple Square where one of them, a pathologically shy puppeteer who called himself Švankmajer, hurried away like a bespectacled hippopotamus from all the Mormons trying to shake his hands and convert him. Later, we retired to the Lion House where Švankmajer ordered a meal of frontier delicacies befitting a polygamist commune. While he silently ate roll after roll slathered in honey butter, those in his entourage discussed the glacier, several of them inviting locals from nearby tables to examine

the icy wounds on their bodies: dendrites growing out of their necks, noses covered in snowflake-like fractals, and even one child whose teeth were entirely ice. I did my best to explain the glacier to the incredulous Czechs. It was ice, but it was something else too: the swirls of turquoise and hypnotic flatness, meltwater ponds and hoar frost which advanced year after year despite the fact snow didn't fall anymore—the glacier was human, the ice the residue of bodies which had, in the nature of things, crumbled away from joy. Little moments of happiness and pleasure didn't do much to the bodies out here. Maybe a numbing tingle in the fingertips, or a patch of frost on your knee.

It was joy you had to worry about. The deep, stabbing bliss. Joy was what caused husbands to wake up and find husbands a heap of ice, or mothers at the playground suddenly itchy, then brittle, then icicles in the sandbox, nature evening things out, taking back something from those who had stolen so much. Marriages were rare. Births almost non-existent. People feared the human in them. They fashioned reserves of guilt, shame, and indifference as a buffer against the glacier's appetite. But joy is a fickle thing. Sometimes it happened all at once, the body dissolving into a fine, snowy powder, and other times slowly flaking away.

Naturally, scientists were encouraged by the glacier's expansion. We might be able to reverse our climate catastrophes, they said with the monotone optimism of a snail, but only if we continue to feed it our joy. How much were we willing to sacrifice for catastrophe?

My voice was soft and dreamy. Švankmajer rubbed his bald head as if it were a peeled egg before dismissing me with a wave of his hand. Only puppets are magical, he said.

It was late when we finally made it to the glacier. It was not crowded. A naked woman sat in a lotus pose a few hundred feet from the shoreline, her icy shoulders in the first stages of melting. A couple spread a bucket of ice into a thin layer. They stood quietly then walked away.

The Czechs stood in a puzzled awe. They murmured. They did not blink. It was obvious they wanted to touch the glacier. They likely had never seen ice before, what with the scarcity—indeed the rarity—of fresh water across the globe. The Dead Sea was a salt flat. The dusty Nile Highway. The Amazon trough. Sand dunes spread over what was once Lake Victoria seemed like withered nipples. From outer space the Ganges, home to a cemetery of old boats, looked like a frayed jump rope.

Leaning close to me, Švankmajer asked if it was painful. Becoming glacier. Is it painful?

I shrugged. Just walk, I told him as Miss Z told everyone, and the glacier will do the rest.

Švankmajer paced the shoreline for more than an hour, plucking his beard like an anxious polygamist. I'm sorry, he finally said, arms dangling like dead fish, I just don't believe it.

That's the unfortunate thing about Utah, I said with a hint of disenchantment, nobody believes anything.

Švankmajer wandered off to the nearby meltwater pond. For the next several hours he knelt in the brackish water and filmed flies and sketched storyboards on napkins as a new puppet film took shape in his mind. A year from now this will be gone, he said, waving his hand at the glacier. Reality is a tissue of dreams but puppets, he smiled, puppets last forever.

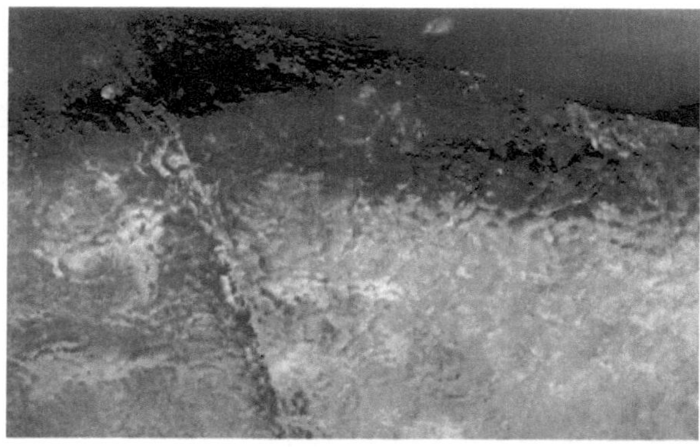

Before leaving, the Czechs looked for their companion who had been lying on the glacier giggling. They found what seemed like the impression of a deformed angel in the ice. They called his name. The sun went down. They quit trying.

I sat on the wobbly kiosk stool until a woman tapped on the window. Is this your shop? she asked. She was pregnant. Her lips were blue and in place of eyebrows grew jagged crystals.

Yes, I lied, my mind snapping like a rubber band out of its reverie.

My husband, she said in a faraway voice as she hoisted a bucket of ice. The world is sick.

She cupped a handful of the husband ice. Traced a finger over the slick edges, pausing as if trying to imagine it was still him. This sliver here not unlike his eye. This dimple here might have been the congenital defect in his heart. This jagged crust like the time he broke a tooth eating popcorn at the movies. I thought of telling her that as ice melts it tessellates. That if you look closely, it forms an almost incomprehensible web of spikes, cones, pyramids, kites, stars, spindles. Nature, like an infirmed fairy tale, has so many shapes.

When she tired of her mental resurrecting, she spilled the handful of husband ice back into the bucket. It crackled. Like he was still talking, speaking in a language none of us understood.

My grandfather had cancer, she said abruptly. He was one of the last. Natural causes. She almost laughed saying it. She found him sitting at his desk, pistol still in his fingers, a small black hole above his temple dripping blood. She was seven.

Goddamn, I'd give anything for that, she said. Anything except this dead not dead.

Yes, I said dreamily, trying not to listen, trying not to imagine with her. I stared at the bucket of ice dripping water, the drips swallowed up by the desert dust. I stared past her into the glacial whiteness.

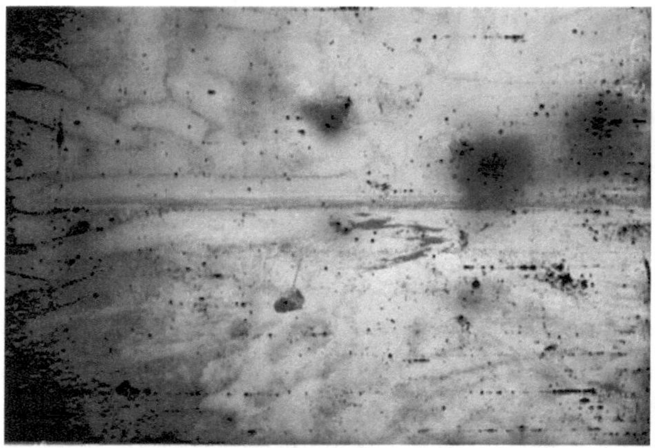

Bookfucker

Dear library patron: According to our records, the material(s) you recently checked out is overdue. Please return said item(s) at your earliest convenience to avoid unnecessary penalties. Forgive us if you have already complied with this request.

Dear library patron: We hope you have enjoyed *Gonorrhea: A Biography*. This notice is to inform you the item in question is past due. Please return said item(s) promptly. Unless remedied, action will be taken. Thank you for supporting literacy.

Dear library patron: We hope you have received our previous notices of the overdue item(s) in your possession. You may be interested to know that today I saw an older man, handsome, a silver fox as they say. The first thing he does when he picks up a book is smell the pages. He will crack the spine to wedge his nose deeper for a more sustained olfactory pleasure. Oh, him? Lucy shrugs, that's just Bookfucker. Waiting at the Circulation Desk I imagine Bookfucker approaching and even though he doesn't ask, I offer my spine for cracking. A book and a woman cannot be so different.

Dear library patron: Did you recently lose a pair of dentures? Lucy discovered them in the bathroom sink following the bi-monthly meeting of the Association for Genital Integrity. No sooner had we posted the sign than elderly patrons appeared asking to try on the missing teeth. We hope you are our Cinderella.

Dear library patron: This is a friendly reminder that the material(s) you recently checked out remains past due. Did it fulfil your needs? Did it exceed your expectations? We hope so. Please remember that borrowing a book is a privilege. Failure to acknowledge this privilege may result in punishments outlined in the contract you signed. Drop boxes remain available for your convenience.

Dear library patron: Lucy wears low-cut tops, glittery pumps, and red lipstick. I wear white sneakers and a cardigan. I want to look grandmotherly. Fashionable people have a 38% increased risk of dementia.

Dear library patron: Would you be so kind as to return *Sokonoff's Theorem*? It is a first edition. Last month, the author came for a book signing. While we were waiting, she explained Sokonoff was her husband and he discovered a mathematical proof that time is an illusion. I laughed and told her sometimes I feel that way working in a library. I never remember arriving or leaving. If I open my eyes I am here. My husband killed himself, the woman said. We stared at the clock.

Dear library patron: There is real pleasure in wandering around a library. I weave between the maze of rows, walk through doors, listen to the echo of my voice in stairwells, crawl inside dumbwaiters. On most days, the geometry of this place suppresses the urge to walk in front of a bus. But I have no particular affection for books. My father read me many bedtime stories, all of which induced sleep. Except Bluebeard. I have always been intrigued by love stories.

Dear library patron: The Circulation Desk is a kind of pornography. Patrons approach sheepishly, like hungry children, eager to watch me inspect pages for defects, caress the spine, titillate the edges with a fingertip. There is a silence between us, and yet there are words. Will you take me into the Civil War history stacks and ski your tongue over my frigid nipples? Receipts and signatures are exchanged. Our transaction finished, I signal for the next patron to approach the counter. It is 9:17 A.M.

Dear library patron: A woman arrives at the library dressed exactly like the Queen of England. As she passes, I curtsy and whisper, *God save you.*

Dear library patron: Today I asked Lucy: You don't think he actually intercourses with books, do you? She smiled, shrugged. Leaning close she whispered, They don't call him Bookfucker for nothing. Later I wondered: how might one fuck a book? Our instruction in middle school Health class was conspicuously nonexistent in this regard. The problem is not as dire as Adam, east of Eden, with Eve lying on the grass beneath him, his eyes alternating between the abyss above and the abyss below. I sneeze. You should take a sick day, Lucy says.

Dear library patron: Somewhere there is a mathematical proof that says the tolerability of other people is directly proportional to the quantity of words leaving their mouth.

Dear library patron: The automatic doors open and the weird wind blows inside. It hisses and whistles and laughs. And then quiet. So much quiet. But it doesn't quit you. You hear it hours later when trying to fall asleep, this mad desert blooming inside your ear. They say if God loves you, he takes you to the desert. The desert, a snake eating its own tail. The desert, where you can love something but that doesn't make it true. The desert, which is sad and beautiful and unreal and is so empty you no longer feel the emptiness inside you.

Dear library patron: A magician performed for the children today. He wore a cape and waved his wand. The children laughed and applauded. I was hoping to see real magic, but his expertise seemed restricted to balloon animals. Has he read *A Brief History of Ballooning*? Perhaps that is where he learned to shape an elephant and umbrella. Perhaps a woman is not so different from a balloon and can be wrapped around a bedpost or twisted on the floor until satisfied with the knot of her own existence. When the children left the magician asked if I wanted to see real magic. I followed him down one of the aisles when suddenly he spun around and kissed me.

Dear library patron: Between the second and third floor is a half floor accessible by a stairwell in the northwest corner. I count six steps. This leads to other stacks and little offices, a library within a library. At the end of the hallway on this half floor is a door nobody opens. That's where Bookfucker goes, Lucy says with a wink. I think she's wrong. I think behind that door is the end of the world.

Dear library patron: To avoid suspension, I complete "Workplace Violence Prevention" training. Apparently, fisting a magician's balls constitutes "violence." Who knew? These two things are equally true: there is no other place in the world I'd rather be than a library, and if only some stranger would hit me senseless with a dictionary.

Dear library patron: As a librarian, I am trained to scrutinize the signatures on the back of library cards to detect fraud. I find handwritten signatures an antiquated tradition and think society would benefit from a more modern form of identification. I would prefer patrons make an identifying mark with their genitals. The testicles of men are quite distinct, as are feminine labia. To be sure, the body is a Rorschach blot. Sometimes I imagine Bookfucker's testicles swatting my cheeks. They are like bearded oranges shriveled from the sun.

Dear library patron: I love the silence of libraries. In a world of radios and television and other babble machines, the library is a sanctuary. Here one may stray into thoughts without the tyranny of making them into words. Thoughts are an intercourse with silence. Words are alphabets of affliction.

Dear library patron: Sometimes I think Bookfucker has figured out a way to avoid this web of words and thoughts. As if fucking is the only way to avoid being fucked.

Dear library patron: My mother was a real furnace of thought. Always a word and smile. She stopped talking after seeing a young woman leap from the highway overpass into oncoming traffic. A produce truck swerved, then flipped, spilling hundreds of watermelons onto the highway. Cars backed up for a mile. A boy and his father were the only victims, both decapitated when they went through the windshield. They found the bodies, but the heads catapulted onto the highway and were lost among the watermelons. A few days later my mother came home carrying one—half-price! she smiled—and I ate until my stomach was round and just a little pink.

Dear library patron: It is easy to forget there are men in the world. They are like the unicorn: pleasant as a picture in a children's book, but disappointing in the flesh. The library is full of women. There are grandmothers, widows, divorcées, fiancées, whores, virgins, housewives and mothers.
Where do so many women find the time to exist?

Dear library patron: You lie, the girl tells her lover. They're in periodicals. She has pink hair and tattoos. He dances on sidewalks all over town waving those GOING OUT OF BUSINESS signs. I've been watching them argue for ten minutes. The boy reaches out to feel her face. She does the same. Until now I have no idea they're blind. I watch them take turns reading the skin like braille. Where else but a library can we find the sadness of bankruptcy and be bankrupted by sadness?

Dear library patron: When I was a girl, I swallowed a nickel. My mom rushed me to the hospital where they took an X-ray. Until then I had no idea I was real. It's a shame nobody can see inside me. There's an awful lot to think about in there. The doctors told me I could watch them cut me open. Count backwards, they said. I made it to six. I woke up with a scar on my belly shaped like the hook of a question mark. It was a dirty trick, one I have not forgiven. Please make time to return the past due items, otherwise your account will be suspended. Despite precautions, mistakes occasionally occur. If you believe an error has been made in your case, please bring to the library—or mail us—this notice and your library card.

Dear library patron: Before my current position, Lucy gave me a tour of the library. She tested me on proper shelving techniques, the Dewey Decimal system, alphanumerics, the mathematics of fiction and nonfiction. Other questions were more difficult: *What are the two acceptable weather patterns? Do you approve of the library's policy on extraterrestrials? If you are alone in a room with two beds, which do you sleep on? What is the first thing you do if the horse you are riding dies?* My score is still the highest of any librarian. When it was over, Lucy gave me a hug. She gave me a set of keys that opened all the doors, even the ones to half-floors. Always knock, she said, you never know what these fuckers are doing behind closed doors.

Dear library patron: A library is a microcosm of democracy. One of our duties is to preserve the sanctity of the books so that freedom may endure. Once a month we inspect the collection. So far, I have found the following inside the books: One slice provolone cheese. Enema tube, used. Forty-seven Russian rubles. Army supply list. Three pubic hairs. Blood test results. Six molars. First-in-show ribbon. Juvenile starfish. Suicide note. Four-leaf clover. Wedding invitation. Bar soap. Sonogram of fetus. Winning lottery ticket. Divorce papers. Why these little seizures of anarchy give me pleasure I cannot say.

Dear library patron: The library is quite cold. Outside the desert sun is a hot blind thing. More and more patrons enter. I used to believe they were escaping the heat, but as I watch them wandering the stacks, I think they come to escape other people. They handle the books carefully, in love with words that say something and nothing at all.

Dear library patron: When was the last time I left the library? I cannot remember. It appears increasingly obvious I am dead and the library is some kind of purgatory, a phase between where we are going and where we have been. My presence here must be a cosmic error, a mistake on the part of some God, but one without rectification. The only way to leave the library, I have determined, is to locate the word that sums up my existence. One word hidden within all these books. Say the word and I will be free of this hell.

Dear library patron: Bookfucker is also searching for his word. This is why he fucks all the books. Fucking is a kind of salvation.

Dear library patron: During story hour the children listened attentively to the tale of Mr. Bluebeard and how he gives his wife a key to every room in the house but makes her promise not to open the door to one special room. Of course, the minute he leaves she waltzes inside and finds the bodies of all his previous wives splattered on the walls. The boys took turns pretending to strangle the girls. One girl didn't want to pretend to be dead and said she was just sleeping until her prince kissed her awake. Very gently I whispered in her ear, *You're living in the wrong story*. She cried.

Dear library patron: The library is a barbaric institution. Would you go to a birthday party, browse through the assortment of children and, selecting one at random, take it home hoping it could feed you, bathe you, clothe you, let it into your secret spaces? Among the ancient Romans unauthorized literacy was punishable by blinding and a month hard labor in the charcuterie trade. Save the date! Next week is the end of the annual Young Readers Summer festival. First prize for most books read is a ribbon along with a coupon for a free basket of onion rings at the Big H. There is still time.

Dear library patron: There is no proof Bookfucker engages in obscene behavior with books. They appear unviolated. Today I watched him. He browsed through a copy of *Crisfeld's Encyclopedia of Peculiar Medical Disorders and How to Cure Them*. I've read that book too. It says prayer is an illness. Is a prayer the same as intercourse? I wanted to ask. When I turned the corner to come up the aisle he was gone. Perhaps he left in a hurry, having discovered something about prayer he wasn't expecting. Later, when the library was almost empty, I tried praying in the same spot where Bookfucker was reading, but nothing happened.

Dear library patron: Bookfucker arrives at precisely 6:00 P.M. We close at 8:00 P.M. He has predetermined which stacks he will visit and with which books he will intercourse. I wonder if punctuality is foreplay or merely a quality of being fucked.

Dear library patron: Toska. Fernweh. Onism. Hyggelig. Ya'aburnee. None of these are my words.

Dear library patron: They say heaven is a library. If this is true, then before we came here God must have rounded up half the spirits and given them a papercut between the thighs. You are women, he said. Sometimes I'll remove a page from a book and give myself a papercut. My thighs and stomach are covered in little white scars. Other times, I stuff wads of paper inside me so one day God may know this body is no longer his to imagine.

Dear library patron: Why do men shake hands and not cocks? This seems like a missed opportunity. After using the toilet, I don't wash my hands. I shake hands with library patrons. It is like losing my virginity over and over.

Dear library patron: Yesterday, between Young Adult Fiction and Young Adult Nonfiction a man showered. He had a bucket and a bar of soap.

Dear library patron: Lucy's specialty is monsters. Mine is romance. We all have our literary gifts. During Halloween she decorates the horror stacks with cardboard cutouts of ghouls, zombies and werewolves. Most of the people who visit that section are pale and fat, like they're hoping a book can intercourse them out of their skin. Lucy reads three horror books a week. That's the thing about monsters, Lucy says, you're never finished with them. She's been writing her own horror story for years. It's about a house. Not a haunted house with ghosts, or a house that comes alive, or even a house that drives people crazy. It's an old house full of dust and mites that slowly kills its occupants with asthma, a house so lonely it induces indigestion. Lucy swallows her pills. Acid reflux is hell, she says.

Dear library patron: Could Bookfucker be the one who complained about the pornography in the library? Good sir, a library is a place of fucked things. Once upon a time we had only our words. But fucking is so magical. Otherwise, we would not have learned how to gut trees and slice them thin and stuff the tree skins into animal skins and ink within this rape all our terribly beautiful thoughts.

Dear library patron: After story hour the children practiced with watercolors. You should have seen their pictures of all the secrets they would keep behind a locked door!

Dear library patron: I stand outside the door and wait for Bookfucker to open. I would not object to being flayed, disemboweled, asphyxiated, even decapitated with my head preserved in an aquarium of formaldehyde. I find these suitable trajectories for any marriage. But I will not be ignored.

Dear library patron: There is a woman who comes on the second Tuesday of every month to lick the pages of the latest *National Geographic* issue. After many months I summoned the courage to ask why she licks the pages and she said, a little embarrassed, that she hoped to taste those faraway places.

Dear library patron: And the mad desert goes on.

Dear library patron: Story hour has been discontinued. The future of democracy is in jeopardy.

Dear library patron: Lucy says Bookfucker's wife died in childbirth and then he gave away the child because the sorrow was too much. There are many fuckers in the world. Bookfucker is just one of them. I do not know what I am. Dear library patron: Our bodies are sixty-eight percent water. We lose fourteen milliliters with every breath. The library has an extensive collection of books on amphibians. Did you know the axolotl, a species of salamander, is terrestrial at birth? As it ages it sheds its legs and returns to the water as a tadpole, maturing into childhood. How often I have walked these library aisles immersed in the problem of our own inadequate evolution.

Dear library patron: Lucy checks out another horror book: *The Algorithms of Happiness*. I tell her about the lice infestation at school when I was a little girl. This place is making you lose your mind, she laughs.

Dear library patron: Today, an old couple built a fort in the middle of the library with pillows and blankets. They lay there quietly whispering about things I can't understand.

Dear library patron: Often during my lunch hour I take the key Lucy gave me and find new places to put it: nostrils, asshole, mouth, ear. Something inside me has opened, but I am not sure what.

Dear library patron: Yesterday, Bookfucker intercoursed with *Modernity and the Napoleonic Imagination*. Looking over the pages I find no trace of Bookfucker's existence. No stains or smudges. No dog-eared pages. No scent. No indication a fucking has occurred. It is like he is a ghost. I do not believe that things unseen are more vital than those we see. I wonder if fucking and ghosting are the same thing.

If Bookfucker were to fuck me, would I be different in a measurable way, or just another footnote in the biography of my life? According to the footnotes, Napoleon was the first to attach a bomb to a balloon. Can you picture the townspeople as the balloon descended? They must have mistaken it for a falling star. We cannot hope to be Napoleons, but we can hope to be balloons.

Dear library patrons: Today, I am made of paper. Bookfucker scrolls me up, takes me to the children's picture books aisle where he unfolds me like a doll, baptizing my clit with his tongue until it gets a paper cut. His tongue bleeds. But I am no Pinocchio. Despite all his efforts, his blood fails to turn my paper into flesh.

Dear library patron: Papercuts are an occupational hazard. Suddenly there it is: a thin slice of flesh. They say on the fingertips is a higher concentration of nerves than an entire elephant's body. And yet a papercut is oddly satisfying. Because they are accidents? I've been brought to my knees by papercuts. They sing, those raw nerves exposed to air. So much pain pressed through such a shallow wound, doing all the things for us that Christ failed to do.

Dear library patron: Just before closing today, a gentleman approached the Help Desk with full makeup on his face. He requested a librarian to help him remove it.

Dear library patron: Once I went to a museum of medical curiosities. There were pickled conjoined twins, genital warts strung on a necklace, jellyfish, amputated fingers. In a display case was a woman's nervous system, carefully dissected from all her flesh, her body arranged like threads spun from some fairy-tale nightmare. Would anybody collect me? I would not object to being skinned. I am pale, unfreckled. They could flay me. Hang me on the third floor like a tapestry next to the skeleton. It was donated by the local biology teacher. It's missing eleven bones and two teeth. We call him George.

Dear library patron: Vemödalen. Jijivisha. Altschmerz. Kairosclerosis. None of these are my words.

Dear library patron: I could hear the paper whimpering all day. Like a foundling crying for its mother's breast. I passed a man in the Natural History aisle watering the books with a flower pot. He smiled. You hear them too?

Dear library patron: Today there was a bomb scare. Lucy says the world is full of wackos and perverts, but she doesn't understand the menace of libraries. This is where we banish all our awful thoughts, our perversions, our secrets—all bound and blotted inside books. Sometimes I imagine a bomb going off, the words escaping their pages, drowning the world in a black river of type.

Dear library patron: That Bookfucker is a real rat, Lucy says, fidgeting with her skirt. To avoid answering her I stare out the window thinking I am a rat and the sun is the Pied Piper. Lately, I stare at the sun for hours. When I close my eyes, I see its shadow. Like a hole or a mouth or an eye. We all know about the hole in the ozone slowly leaking radiation. Oz, Lucy calls it. There's a book about it, but it's always checked out. The old timers who come in say Oz is a lie invented by commie pinko bastards, but there's no doubting the sun. It melts nickels in the gutter. I stare until my eyes sting, but I have to believe the universe is more than a word trying to fuck us. I stare and try to believe in the slow blinding white light of heaven.

Dear library patron: Mamihlapinatapei. Mamihlapiatapei.

Dear library patron: I have not seen Bookfucker in weeks. Perhaps he found his word. If so, I am happy for him. Perhaps there is no book of life on the shelf for me, just words doomed to float like castaways on the ocean of my mind. I do not know. I am comforted by the hope there are still hallways and nooks in the library with other women like me. Satisfied. Unfulfilled.

Dear library patron: It is with great sadness that we had to suspend the account of one of our patrons. It could happen to you too. We caught her tearing out pages from the books and turning them into paper cranes. Senbazuru, she told us. One thousand origami birds held together by string. If I finish them, I said, the gods will grant me a wish. But you're not Japanese, Lucy told me. Later, after Lucy goes home, I finish folding the last paper crane and put it in the desk drawer. The next morning, the paper crane is gone.

Dear library patron: Please disregard all previous correspondence. There has been a clerical error. The items have been successfully renewed. Thank you for your patronage.

Of Angels

I never saw my grandmother's great-great-grandmother, Arlytia Carter Habermeyer, make love to an angel. It happened at Locust Creek. Her husband, Martin Horton Habermeyer, a gifted trumpeter in the Mormon Battalion who had no idea what to do with those lips, tried to defend his wife's virtue by challenging the angel to a wrestling match. She died in childbirth.

I never saw her grandson, James Ernst Habermeyer, waiting in Sundance canyon at midnight to trade his soul to play the fiddle. The angel convinced him there is a devilry beyond music and it's called dentistry.

Rosanna Josephine Habermeyer saw angels on top of the Salt Lake tabernacle drinking tea.

Ebenezer Hyrum Habermeyer heard angels laughing at Mountain Meadows.

I never saw the angel visit Eugene Cyrus Habermeyer who suffered from a gangrenous toe. They got on a train to San Francisco and were never seen again.

Murray Ansel Habermeyer saw angels melting ants with a magnifying glass.

Heber van Orden Habermeyer saw angels bathing in the Spanish Fork hot springs. They sang Italian opera with flawless accents.

I never saw Florence May Habermeyer the winter before the winter they outlawed polygamy eavesdropping at the quilting bee on the *squirrelish but earnest* lovemaking of angels. She aborted nine little ones.

I never saw the angel appear to Effie Sophronia Habermeyer during the drought of 1907 and supply her with lozenges of laudanum. She sold them for a handsome profit to nervous housewives.

Olive Emilia Habermeyer saw an angel lose a tooth in a game of Mormon basketball.

Phineas Cannon Habermeyer, a sailor, shared a urinal with a guardian angel in Cuba. Nothing ever happens these days, the angel complained.

Lovinia Mabel Habermeyer, who brought coffee to Oppenheimer at Los Alamos, saw angels writing equations on blackboards. Their bodies glowed pale orange.

My grandmother, Esther Elisabeth Habermeyer, told her daughters to be little guardian angels and wait outside while she paid the piano teacher. Forty years later my aunts mulled DNA tests.

My mother, Sharlene Joanne Habermeyer, who is too afraid to verify her paternity, saw angels teaching people falling from the South Tower how to spread their arms and fly.

My son started believing in angels after his wife died. It happened in a laundromat off Highway 59. It looked less like an angel and more like one of those Roswell Gray aliens on the *X-Files* with the bulbous head and black, pupil-less eyes. The angel put on my dead daughter-in-law's clothes, slowly, like a reverse strip tease. I never saw my son put his hand on the angel's potbelly, or the angel stretch its webbed fingers over my son's chest. Two widowers. Oh, what a sad fucking cosmos.

I never asked him why he sold his story to the *National Enquirer*, or what he does with those fan letters saying they've spotted an angel in drag driving a Chevy Malibu with a bumper sticker that says HEAVEN IS SAD.

Whispering rainbows. Jellyfish weddings. Babies with glass skin. It helps to believe in the impossible things, things so invisible they have to be real. I don't, but it helps. Things like angels circling the tub as I was under the water, waiting for the air to run out. I thought it was the rapture. Only I didn't die, but I wasn't saved either.

The Inheritors

Once a month, the dining center at the Bodhitree Retirement Community offers exotic meat Mondays. Octopus tacos. Rattlesnake kabobs. Even kangaroo burgers. Formerly a ghost town, the recently converted community resides on forty-four square miles of pristine desert just outside of Kanab. It is the number four facility in the state of Utah, preferred three-to-one by citizens of advanced age. Mr. Meh-Teh avoids exotic meat Mondays. There is nothing puritanical about it. It is simply that Mr. Meh-Teh is a Yeti and seeing so many residents shoveling exotic meats down their throats makes him a little uncomfortable.

———

Mr. Meh-Teh stands outside the recreation center. He stares at his hand opening and closing. He has hairy knuckles. The door handle is smudged with fingerprints. Mr. Meh-Teh, the Yeti, last known of his kind, has opposable thumbs. He has often wondered about them. Did they just appear one morning on the hands of a distant relative? Or was it a work-in-progress, these strange thumbs which slowly twisted into position? He moves the thumb around and around in a circular motion as he feels the ligaments and muscles tighten and slack. This too is strange: that something so evolved as a thumb moves in circles. Sometimes he would throw snowballs at the Pangboche monks during their meditations, hoping to rattle them out of wherever they were projecting their consciousness. He knows how to use his hands. But he hesitates with the door. He wants to go inside but he also does not want to be inside. Two gentlemen brush past him. It's a door, dumbass, a man grunts. He's bald and wears a plaid shirt tucked into pleated khakis. His friend sneers at the Yeti. Yeah, he's quick as a glacier, the man laughs. The two walk away. The Yeti knows he's not as sharp as he once was. His hairs have turned from white to gray. His testicles droop. His teeth are dulled. The arthritis in his big toe makes it difficult to walk and gives him bad posture. The Yeti ignores the men, hiding behind the perception he has a rudimentary vocabulary. He doesn't want trouble. His visa is stamped RESIDENT ALIEN and he fears deportation. He could go ape on them. Beat his chest. Snarl. Fling shit. He remembers listening to stories of how his ancestors preyed on *Homo erectus*. Shit-sniffers, they were called. The Yeti is not docile by nature. A hundred thousand years of evolution cannot be unlearned in a lifetime, but the Yeti remembers the meditation practices he discovered spying on the Pangboche monks. He relaxes his jaw, breathes deeply, and imagines blue glaciers.

———

Tonight is therapy in the Dharma room. The Yeti is the reluctant star of therapy. Non-compulsory attendance has doubled since he arrived. They come for him, for the carnival sideshow. It doesn't matter that the Yeti uses the appropriate utensils during meals, knows the best wine pairing for stewed lamb is a Languedoc red, and can recite from memory the aphorisms of Benjamin Franklin. They come to see if the Yeti is a missing evolutionary link or some terrible lab experiment. The Yeti used to believe solitude was a punishment before being forced into retirement. Exile. Retirement. Is there a difference? the Yeti wonders. He has since learned company is its own kind of misery. He longs for privacy. He longs for a mountain of snow with nothing but his footprints following him. It's exhausting having to live up to a mythology he never asked for. Confessions are mild tonight. Mrs. Yorgensen admits to being a nymphomaniac and requests an orgy with the men in Unit C. Mr. Kimball wants to change his DNR policy again. Mrs. Talbot insists the orderlies are videotaping her in the shower and posting it on the web tube. There are the usual complaints of negligent children and lousy mattresses. There is a stipulation in the Yeti's visa that requires his participation in therapy. Failure to do so may or may not result in additional deportations and rehabilitative assignments. The Yeti has often thought about violating the terms of his visa. After hundreds of years of solitude, he has no interest in retirement, which is just a different kind of ice age. Don't tell them anything, the Yeti remembers Maggie Benson whispered during his first week in therapy. Maggie had frazzled gray hair that at one time suggested she had been every young boy's fantasy. Now it was just sad, and she seemed aware of this. The Yeti scrunched his face. It's a death panel, Maggie said. Don't you know? That's what these places are—a cemetery for the living, she said. Maggie died two weeks after the Yeti arrived. She was eighty-two.

———

After therapy there are arts and crafts. Today is animal hide fabric day. Everyone gets a few pieces of leather. The men make wallets. One old bird named Mavis stitches a mask with slits for eyeholes and a zipper for the mouth. She presses it into the Yeti's hand. Come to my dorm and see the rest of it, Mavis whispers, sticking out her well-endowed chest. Unit D. Mavis has thirty-eight grandchildren. They visit infrequently. Her husband was a drunk and she has offered to marry the Yeti in a Mormon ritual so they can ascend to the third heaven and have little Yeti babies in the afterlife. The Yeti stands in the doorway and uses oversized hands to zip and unzip the zipper, wondering if humans will one day evolve a zipper for a mouth.

———

There are Mormons making arts and crafts. Two sunburnt twenty-somethings in dress slacks and ties like used car salesmen, both mysteriously answering to the name Elder. A fat one and a skinny one. They call themselves missionaries. They're here every week, supposedly to volunteer, but all they really do is eat free desserts and try to save the Yeti's soul. Until the missionaries told him he had one the Yeti never considered a soul was good for much of anything. The skinny missionary told the Yeti he had an old soul. You're Cain, brother Meh-Teh, the skinny missionary said. Apparently, a long time ago the Yeti killed his brother and was cursed to walk the earth forever. Now the Mormon god had sent these sunburnt boys to save him. This surprised the Yeti. Not that God was looking for him, but that everyone has an explanation for him except himself. He wants to believe there might be something divine about these clueless boys. He wants to believe the skinny one who says the Yeti needs a special Mormon bath, a baptism, if he is to receive his celestial inheritance. Don't roll the dice with Buddhism, the skinny one tells the Yeti while taking a bite of his doughnut, because with reincarnation you might come back a silkworm. Or worse, he leans in and whispers, a Catholic.

Nobody can pronounce the Yeti's name. *Meh-Teh*, the Yeti says. Oh, you worked for the Maytag company? Mrs. Yorgensen says, trying to stitch together the leather. Wonderful washing machines. She leans forward. I'll tell you what I told the bishop's wife but never the bishop. When my husband went away on business trips, she says, I made sure he forgot his electric toothbrush. Her eyes get wide. Perfectly filled cavities, she winks. *Meh-Teh*, the Yeti says. Mai tais taste like shit, a man with oxygen tubes in his nostrils says. He leans back from his puzzle and folds his arms across his chest. Real men drink bourbon, he says, no ice. The Yeti misses ice. He remembers when the geologist from the oil and gas company tried to recruit him. The ice is vanishing, he told the Yeti. In a few years there'll be nothing left. The geologist and his friends promised if the Yeti led them through the caves, if he showed them where to find the oil and gas, they would give him a house and a 401(k) and an ice-maker for all the ice he could ever desire. Instead, the Yeti took them to see the glaciers. He had them stand in that silence and look at how water can be blue and white and green all at once. He must be retarded, the oil men said. His favorite thing now is to take an ice cube from the freezer and stand on the patio in this awful desert. He likes the feeling of the melting ice, each hexagonal crystal dissolving as it collapses on its neighbor. It takes only a few minutes. He used to loathe the snow. Snow in his fur, between his toes, freezing his lips and numbing his balls. Now watching the ice dissolve makes the Yeti homesick. He used to sit in the Himalayas and watch the glaciers melt in a slow, steady drip. Other times the ice thickened in monstrous waves. He listened to the glaciers move. They made a curious sound, like notes of a piano out of tune. Sometimes the Yeti spends all night melting ice from the freezer. He closes his eyes and dreams he is somewhere else awaiting the next great Ice Age, trying to fall in sync with the music of glaciers.

In an adjoining room there is a subcommittee session for those involved in the constipation protest. Dr. Wambaugh has been discouraging it for weeks. Dr. Wambaugh is the director. She arranged for the Yeti's relocation and insists the Bodhitree Retirement Community is a respectable facility and not a circus sideshow. Dr. Wambaugh wears cream-colored slacks and a lab coat. Her hair is pinned up and reveals the back of her neck, smooth like the inside of an olive. Enthusiasm for the constipation rally is waning. A few banners have been made. But the participants are tired. Mr. Turley says he shit last night after four days of resistance. Mrs. Pulsipher caved this morning. Even the more militant residents—men like Lenny Meacham, a retired electrician from Tooele—speak with weary fanaticism. Someday we'll shit like we used to, the way God intended us, he tells the rest of the group, tugging at the elastic band on his regulation diaper. Everyone wears them. The constipators have tried to recruit the Yeti to their cause. Aren't ya a Buddhist? Isn't non-violent aggression what you people do? someone asks. The Yeti looks away. He does not fully understand these human animals. They seek validation for every little thing. Everybody knows the Yeti does not wear the regulation diapers. Everybody knows he refuses to use the toilet and, after curfew, takes a walk into the desert when he wants a constitutional. He will not compromise this instinct. If he does, the Yeti believes, then he will have to own this life. Dr. Wambaugh assures the constipators the Yeti has no interest in their childish displays. Isn't that right, Mr. Meh-Teh? she smiles. The Yeti mumbles. He is confident this is the way America will end: not with a bomb, but with a group therapy circle.

In the rec room the Yeti watches a documentary on yetis. There is footage of footprints in the snow and blizzards with blurry shapes followed by high-pitched cries. The more footage he sees the less he believes he exists. The Yeti knows he exists but would like to *know* he exists. The Yeti takes a Xanax.

Can we pray with you before leaving, brother Meh-Teh? the skinny missionary asks. The Yeti shrugs. The skinny missionary bows his head. Thank you, father in heaven, for the moisture we have received. Please send us more. More importantly, please water the faith of our lost brother, Mr. Meh-Teh, wandering the wilderness of doubt. Help him know he's not alone. The Yeti does not understand Mormon prayers. The Pangboche monks took vows of silence. Words were a sickness. They listened. To the breeze, the water, the earth. To nothing. They tried to harmonize themselves with the world around them. But the Mormon god wants his people to stick out like a sore, opposable thumb. As far as the Yeti can tell, the Mormon god is a bearded cosmonaut floating on an interstellar harem who demands a one-year supply of potato pearls and sends his angels to repair flat tires for stranded motorists. There is something beautiful about a god who listens to his creations. There is something beautiful about a god who demands worship of the invisible. There is something frightening about a god like that too.

The Yeti is folding his laundry when the women walk into the room. No, no, they say, you've done it all wrong again. See the wrinkles here? That will never do. Take these off, honey, they say, tugging at his trousers. The Yeti stands in the laundry room in his undergarments and lets the women paw him. *Meh-Teh*, the Yeti tries to protest, indicating with his hands he has this under control. People always expect a yeti to look like a mongoloid ape, but the Yeti is more complicated than that. He is hairy and unkempt and misshapen, but his hands and face are strangely familiar. His palms are especially soft and forgiving. While one of the women irons his shirts three others groom him. They oil scissors and comb the tangles in his fur. They apply conditioners. They pick out burs and lice and ticks, squishing the creatures between their fingers. The Yeti prefers to squish the lice between his fingertips but preserve the ticks. He is not sure why. Perhaps there is something admirable about a species that can disembody and still survive. Mavis trims the fur around his navel. Her shirt is low cut and the Yeti can see the shaded furrow between her heavy breasts. It is a primal pose. The Yeti has often wondered what Mavis expects of him. He is a foreigner, displays an uncertain biological condition, and he may or may not be thousands of years old—the aging process for yetis is different than humans—but he showers daily, keeps his nails filed, polishes his teeth and scents his fur. He has visited the Bodhitree Community library and read *The Joy of Sex*. The first month after his arrival he seldom left his dormitory, preferring to watch late-night infomercials and order cosmetic products on clearance from QVC. He still has a tube of NoWangAway warming ointment made in China. Unused, sadly. But despite a few thousand years of instinct, he is not exactly sure what to do with a woman with thick-rimmed glasses and a Southwestern accent. The entourage of women is chatty. They remind him of the sanitation crew that deloused him after he was discovered in a Himalayan cave. The Yeti was performing his afternoon mantras when a heavy-set man with a clipboard strolled inside. He was a geologist from an oil and gas company prospecting for hydrocarbons. When the Yeti stepped out from the shadows with his animal pizzle dangling between his legs the geologist's face twisted with horror and fascination. You're trespassing, the geologist said. *Meh-Teh*, the Yeti said. The Yeti spent the night in a Nepalese detainment cell. They placed him under twenty-four-hour surveillance because they suspected he was not toilet trained. Three months later a government committee, under the direction of the oil company, designated the Yeti for rehabilitation. They signed the paperwork and put him on the first plane to Utah, assuring him how lucky he was to live the American dream. Still too many wrinkles, one of the women says, tugging at the Yeti's trousers. Take them off again, she says. Slowly, the Yeti unbuckles his belt, trying not to think too deeply about why clothes feel like a monstrous costume. The women lather their hands with shaving cream and apply it to his chest. The Yeti does not protest this humiliation. He does not howl and beat his chest and say fuck this shit, I'm the Yeti. He loves the touch of their hands, but their fingers make him burn hot with shame. Once shaved, his skin is soft and pinkish, like a newborn infant.

———

At 10:00 P.M. sharp the lights go out. Orderlies patrol the halls to make sure nobody wanders. Protocol dictates twenty-four-hour surveillance. *For your peace of mind*, the brochures say. Grown-up children taking a tour of the facility, eager for their inheritance, smile when they hear this and quickly sign the paperwork to enroll their parents. The facility is built on an old ghost town. There are seventeen domestic units, each with five floors, each floor with fourteen dormitories and a maze of hallways and stairwells and doorways exactly like the other. The Yeti does not like to sleep. He prefers wandering. If he falls asleep, he might never wake up. He's seen it happen. The past smooths away like peanut butter spread over bread leaving a pile of crumbs waiting to be swept off the table. To distract the residents from the breadcrumbs of their lives the facility provides neatly packaged activities advertised in the weekly catalog: *Please join us for the bi-monthly Shuffle Board Tournament. Doubles and singles welcome. Equipment provided. Those with preexisting medical conditions must secure approval from Dr. Wambaugh.* Death is advertised on invitation cards that arrive almost daily: *Services held tomorrow. Shuttle available to and from the chapel. Light refreshments will be served.*

The Yeti does not understand his own mind. Now that he is alone the Yeti feels terribly lonely and faced with the same dilemma: he has never been happier, and he has never been more miserable. He wishes he had spoken with one of the laundry ladies. Maybe held her hand in his, if only for a few seconds. If he concentrates, he can still feel their breath on him. It warms him. It makes him sick. Suddenly, there's a knock on the door. It's Euline. She's the only one who hasn't tried to convince the Yeti he must be baptized. She holds out an extra portion of dessert. I won't tell if you won't, Euline smiles. The Yeti, who knows very well what to do with Euline but is too afraid to come out from behind the door, shakes his head and offers a conciliatory wave of his hand. He prefers to be alone, he gestures. Lying in bed, the Yeti cannot understand why he said what he said. He opens the front door expecting to see Euline still waiting for him, but the hallway is empty. In the doorway are leftover crumbs from the clandestine dessert. The Yeti gathers them in his palm, haunted by their smallness.

The Yeti watches endless amounts of television. His first month he discovered advertisements for psychic hotlines. They spoke in riddles like Buddhist monks. Once the bill arrived his phone privileges were revoked. He has moved on to game shows and PBS documentaries. Tonight, there is investigative reporting on the illegal gorilla trade in Uganda. There are interviews with activists and poachers. There are photographs of half-naked children sitting on a pyramid of gorilla carcasses. They are so small. In another photograph a village constructs a wall from bleached gorilla skulls. Villagers smile. Other bones are fashioned into utensils and fertilizers, sometimes grounded into powder and administered as an aphrodisiac. It is wondrous and terrifying, this television, the Yeti thinks. Anything can suddenly appear. Something beautiful. Something horrible. The Yeti wishes he were a psychic and knew what the television would tell him next. When he cannot watch any more the Yeti turns off the television and stands hunched in the living room. His neck has a knot from constantly bending over to avoid the light fixture. The architects did not consider the needs of a Yeti when crafting their designs and the Yeti has difficulty wedging himself through doorways, his feet often slipping on the slick tile. The Yeti enjoys the dark. All the images from the television fade away and it is quiet. In the darkness life slows down. He misses that slowness. There are too many cars, cables, highways, wires, invisible waves, and other transmissions to keep track of these days. He stands in the darkness, unsure whether to close his eyes or open them. He turns the television back on so he doesn't have to be alone, but the longer he watches the more alone he feels.

———

The Yeti prefers to defecate under the mesquite brush. He refuses to use the toilet. It is so unnatural. Tonight, the Yeti digs a bowl of dust at the roots. He does not relieve himself. He stands and admires the hollowed-out earth. He would like to fling his shit, maybe howl, but feels ashamed at the thought of it. It is an odd routine, but it gives him inexplicable satisfaction to carry on the evolutionary urges. At night, the Utah desert is haunting. The wind howls and threatens to bury everything in dust. It is a reminder that one day soon the Yeti will be dust. Maybe, he thinks, he belongs here with the dust, even if he knows he can never belong anywhere. It was much easier in the Himalayas. He had snow. He had the Pangboche monks. Now there are Mormons and dust. Wandering over hills he thinks he sees his cousin, the Sasquatch. He waves. As he hurries closer his chest tightens with disappointment. It is only a juniper tree. At his deportation hearing the Yeti was promised valleys and streams and conjugal visits at the gorilla exhibit in a nearby zoo. He was promised something better than snow—snow cones. Sitting on a juniper branch, all desire slowly leaks out into the dust and is quickly buried in other dusts.

———

The Yeti waits in a parking lot watching the stars. There is a woman not far from here, the most famous woman in town, who was lying on her couch one evening when a meteorite crashed through her roof and hit her on the stomach. It left a bruise shaped like the Milky Way. The local Mormons said the meteor was from Kolob, the star where God lives with his wives. They took her photograph for the newspaper and interviewed her for television. Someone wrote a song about her. People came from a hundred miles away just to touch the bruise. The Yeti is wondering whether he too is a kind of meteorite when he sees the fat missionary on the other end of the parking lot. He's barefoot. The tie dangles loosely around his neck. The Yeti wants to talk to him, but hunches down on the curb hoping to make himself another shadow. The missionary walks towards him. The Yeti gets a knot in his stomach. What will they talk about? Ask him what he's doing this late at night, ask him why he's not with his skinny friend because they always travel in pairs? Maybe the Yeti will ask to know more about himself. Jesus, the fat missionary says, you don't look good. Want a cigarette? The Yeti shakes his head. The missionary asks if the Yeti is going to tell on him. The Yeti grunts, confused. Me and the other elder are never supposed to be out of each other's sight, the missionary says. Never supposed to be alone. Can you imagine having someone always breathing down your neck? Never being alone? Jesus, the fat missionary says shaking his head. The Yeti stares at the black nametag the fat missionary wears. ELDER BAUM, it says. I like the stars. I like being alone with them, the missionary says. He presses on his temples like there is an ache. Have a smoke, he says. The Yeti gags when he first inhales. It tastes earthy and sour, almost like the leaves the Pangboche monks used to burn. Almost like home. Feel better? the missionary asks. The Yeti shakes his head. The two of them stare at the stars. Do you believe in God? the fat missionary asks. No, I guess you wouldn't. Can't blame you. Not easy believing in God if you're looking in the mirror, friend. I wouldn't if I were you. Fuck, look at you. And mirrors? God shouldn't have created those either. I mean, what was he thinking? What kind of God makes something like you? A child with a chemistry set. If there's you, well, then there must be mermaids and if there's mermaids there are unicorns and thanks but no thanks. That's one miracle too many. The fat missionary takes a long drag on the cigarette. You've got to have a lot of heart to create something like you, he says. Gods with big hearts scare the shit out of me. I bet you have a big heart. That's the only way you've made it this far. You ever listen to your own heartbeat? Don't. Trust me. Sometimes it's like a clap of thunder and other times a pebble skipped on a lake. Thunder, that's no big deal. But hiccups? Shit. You're a hiccup of nature. Once I hiccupped for six months straight. Doctors didn't know what was happening. I thought I was dying. Finally, the bishop put his hands on my head to cast out the hiccups in the name of Jesus and you know what? He said amen and I hiccupped. That's when I knew I didn't believe any of it, you know, the missionary says. Gods, Mormons, a life after this one. Well, I believe it, but I don't believe it. I want to believe it, but I don't want to believe it. Shit, he shakes his head. You know what I'm saying? I never asked for any of this, the missionary says. Nobody asked me. You're just born with it. Who decides what you're born with and what you get to believe? Not me. Well, I'm here to get away, the fat missionary says. He tells the Yeti his parents didn't want him to be a missionary. They were afraid of what might happen if he was alone. They used to believe. They used to be in love and dance in the kitchen. Now the only time they are romantic is when they say *fuck you* in the hallway. I had to get away, the fat missionary says. You ever feel that way? Like you want to be far away from something but the farther you get the closer it is? God, I wish I could believe. But faith is smaller than a hiccup, and it's the small things that ruin you, friend. Trust me. Smiles. Ladybugs. Stars. My mother's voice when she cries. Salmon eggs. Bubbles. A grain of sand. Shit. A prophet once said we should find heaven in a grain of sand. Can you believe it? Heaven? Probably as fucked up as this place. Who wants to inherit that eternity? Do you? *Meh-Teh*, the Yeti says.

Before returning to his dormitory the Yeti brings a bottle of aged bourbon to the gas station clerk. Most of the locals refuse to offer the Yeti services. They are of two minds. Either he is some idiot kid in an abominable snowman costume, or he is some pervert hipster who didn't get the memo about shaving. Welcome home, the clerk says with a sly grin. The Yeti does not understand the American humor. He mumbles something about not being from here, his voice barely registering above a whisper. Shit, you could have fooled me, the clerk says. You look like all the rest singing in a Sunday pew. The Yeti sits on the curb. Already, he misses the fat missionary. He takes long swigs from the bottle. His throat burns. No wonder the human animals have twisted faces and are always yelling. He used to sit in the trees and watch the Pangboche monks distill Raski in large vats. When inebriated the monks would twist each other's nipples to see who could endure the most pain. The Yeti longed to drink Raski and have his nipples twisted. Sometimes he will bring a bottle of liquor back to his dormitory and drink it in the dark while twisting his own nipple and chanting his mantras. When finished, the Yeti throws the bottle in a ditch. He wonders how long it will be before the desert erodes away and they uncover Atlantis. He cannot be the only one. In some other part of the country a mermaid must be working as a waitress in a sushi bar. It is lonely being the only freak. But the Yeti also wants to be alone. Sometimes, right before he falls asleep, he dreams of finding another yeti hiding within one of the sandstone caves. He pictures them making love. Other times he pictures himself strangling the other yeti so he can be the only one. He cannot decide which is the dream and which is the nightmare.

———————

The Yeti watches a girl pump gas. She is uncomfortably pregnant. With one hand she balances the nozzle and in the other arm holds a young baby. The Yeti spent so many years longing for contact with these human animals now that he is surrounded by them he doesn't know what to do. They laugh, they cry, they yell, they remain silent. So many emotions. The Yeti has much to learn. He fidgets on the curb wondering if he should talk to her. She might be nice. She might be nasty. The Yeti offers to pump her gas. The pregnant girl smiles. The baby squeals playfully at the sight of the Yeti. It makes his heart beat fast. He feels an odd camaraderie to these animals, these humans, like he is staring in the mirror only the reflection is not quite the image he expects. After pumping the gas, the Yeti washes her windows and checks the tire pressure. Rummaging through his pockets the Yeti produces a candy bar which he offers to the baby. The baby falls into his arms with ease. He pops the hood and shows the baby the serpentine belt. The baby puts his finger up the Yeti's nostril, licks it, and giggles. When the Yeti returns to the front seat the pregnant girl is asleep. He nudges her with his paw. She apologizes and tries to give the Yeti some money. Coins fall from her hand and in his effort to pick them up the Yeti accidentally snags the girl's dress with his fingers. It rips. The Yeti, cheeks flushed with humiliation, opens his arms in an effort to apologize which the girl mistakes as an assault. Pervert! she screams, slapping the Yeti's face. In her frantic movements she twists the Yeti's nipples. The Yeti grunts. The baby is crying. The Yeti loses his balance and tumbles forward, pressing the pregnant girl onto her back. In his panic, the Yeti accidentally scratches her thigh. There is blood. The baby is crying. The pregnant girl screams. The Yeti wonders if this is how the woman screamed when God's star crashed through her roof. The Yeti lies very still on the ground and covers his ears, doing his best impression of a glacier.

———

The sheriff and his deputies keep the Yeti handcuffed and face-down on the curb while they take a statement from the pregnant girl. She is pale and trembling. When she looks at the Yeti she faints. A deputy opens the Yeti's paper sack. He sniffs. You bringing sand nigger drugs into my town asshole? Hey, I'm talking to you, brownie, the deputy says. *Meh-Teh*, the Yeti whispers. You're going to be the belle of the ball, one of the deputies whispers in the Yeti's ear. It's not every day they get an exotic piece of ass. The sheriff tells the deputy to shut his mouth. This sonfabitch has rights like the rest of them, the sheriff says. He does? the deputies squint. Even the Yeti is surprised to hear this. Yep, the sheriff says, he has the right to shine my shoes. The sheriff kicks the Yeti in the jaw. The Yeti pisses himself. Baptism by fire, the deputies laugh. The Yeti is suddenly unsure if he exists. The pain reminds him he does, but the pain also sends his mind drifting into the emptiness of space. He feels himself floating there. It frightens him. He tries to claw his way back. Another kick makes him howl. If only he didn't exist. The Yeti could protest this injustice. But why bother? It is not that words are useless, but that the future has already been written. Having arrived in his old age the Yeti no longer knows whose story he is in, only that it is not his own. The lines have been scripted and the pages published, and he is merely an actor performing the fantasy required of him. No amount of prayers or shit-flinging or stargazing will change that. The sheriff stomps the Yeti in the balls. He shits himself.

———

In the morning, the Yeti is released from the county jail and ordered to appear in court within thirty days. Before returning to his dormitory, he walks to the store. Male hygiene products are on sale. He gave up using his tongue a long time ago. Now the Yeti prefers to use a loofah. Only animals like washcloths. The Yeti has a difficult time selecting the proper loofah. There are dozens of colors. Some have handles and others do not. Some loofahs are made especially for backs, others for faces, many for elbows. Many are knit tightly to appear like a piece of hollowed corn, and others fit on the hand like a glove. There are pads and scrubbers and discs and slippers and buffs. The loofah fabric can be tough like sandpaper or spongy like a sea creature. There are Egyptian loofahs, Indonesian loofahs, even Mayan loofahs. The Yeti searches but is disappointed there is no Tibetan loofah.

The Yeti stands in the aisle and feels exhausted. He wants to ask for help but worries about the kinds of questions he might be asked. Human animals are very fickle. There was a time when the Yeti was fond of choices. When he first explored his cave in the Himalayas he was seized with the thrill of discovery. Iced stalactites hung like errant teeth. He wandered deeper and deeper under the mountain labyrinth, creating a detailed map in his mind. It excited him to come to a dead-end and retrace his steps, always finding something new, something different. The Yeti petitions one of the Mega-Mart employees to assist him in selecting a loofah for sensitive skin. He explains he has never visited a dermatologist for a proper consultation. The employee looks at the rows of loofahs, then stares at the Yeti with raised eyebrows. Shit. Does it really matter, dude?

———

The Yeti watches the orderlies with their flashlights circle the facility. They are constantly reminding the residents: Nobody allowed out of their rooms between 10:00 PM and 5:00 AM or the Bear Lake Monster will carry you away. They don't joke like that with the Yeti. Stay inside or we'll send you home, asshole, they say. The Yeti knows he can't go back home. With the oil spills and melting glaciers there is no home. There is only *Meh-Teh*.

———

The Yeti passes slowly through the quad at the retirement center. The constipation crowd is busy preparing for the protest. Lenny Meacham hangs a banner above a doorway. FECAL FREEDOM! There are others. CLEAN OUR CLOTHES, NOT OUR COLONS. EMPATHY, NOT ENEMAS. Lenny asks the Yeti what he thinks. The Yeti does not have the heart to tell him the sadness of it all. A farmer walks through the quad with a herd of goats. It is pet therapy day. Every month there is a new social activity. The state legislature, in conjunction with the medical board of trustees, has decreed that the elderly require stimulating contact. Sometimes kindergarten classes are bused in for an afternoon. Once the community was treated to a theatrical reenactment of the Mountain Meadows Massacre. Animal shelter representatives arrive with dogs and cats. The pet store owner brings lizards and rare birds from halfway across the world. The residents get to groom, feed, walk, and pet the animals. Only the Yeti seems to realize this is psychological conditioning so the residents do not revolt when the staff groom, feed, walk, and bathe them.

The Yeti visits the infirmary. We have some helpers today, the nurse says. It's the fat missionary and his skinny friend. The missionaries help bathe the Yeti. It feels pleasant to have his skin scrubbed with the loofah. At the same time, it feels horrible being this vulnerable. The Yeti keeps his eyes down, afraid to look at the fat missionary. When he does, it's like the fat missionary doesn't see him at all. Baum. Baum, he wants to say, but doesn't. The Yeti stands at the mirror while the nurse dabs his cuts and bruises with disinfectant. He mumbles. He can still taste the blood in his mouth. It takes an hour for the fat missionary to comb the tangles out of his matted fur. The skinny one oils him in lavender and applies a generous handful of tea tree lotion. This isn't the way he imagined life, with cuticles that need moisturizing and arthritic paws, but maybe nobody gets the life they pray for. The last order of business is the toilet. The nurse insists. The Yeti mumbles in protest of this humiliation. The fat missionary takes him by the hand and helps the Yeti squat over the toilet. The porcelain is cold and causes him to shiver. He can feel his heart swelling in his throat, his heart hiccupping like a ghostly thing. The fat missionary's hands are also cold and the Yeti trembles as he is wiped clean. That wasn't so difficult, was it? the fat missionary says. He helps the Yeti into one of the regulation diapers, then steps back to admire his handiwork. There, you see? the fat missionary says. Now you're one of us.

Delousing

Walk through the doors in six-inch heels and the pimple-boy behind the counter says, *Welcome to Big H, home of the pastrami burger with a runny egg*, and I tell him if I don't get some fry sauce my head will explode. *You got a bomb?* pimple-boy stutters as he steps back from the register real slow.

Customers look worried. Like they don't know if it's a joke or my last fuck to give. Maybe I got a bomb. Maybe I don't. The Big H is good eating, explosive diarrhea good, but not spontaneous combustion good. *Fry sauce*, I tell the Zitmeister, taking out my lipstick and holding it like a detonator. *Fresh and thick. None of that thinned-out piss.*

Lately, some things have happened. The cat spent four lives falling out the window. Scratchers didn't scratch. Botched dine and dash at the Benihanas. There was a pain in my spleen circuit which the doctor insists is imaginary. I'm agnostic, I say. There's your problem, she says, and slides two fingers inside me.

Halfway through my set at the Exotic Kitty, the school calls to say there's been an outbreak. *Don't worry*, they say, *this time it's only lice.* Standing outside we watch as the children come marching single-file like miniature soldiers in their blue polos and plaid skirts. Only headless. Where each child's head should be is a jagged, bloody stump. Stumbling through the doors, they wave.

Later, I tour the gymnasium where the heads are being quarantined. They're arranged on stools in neat rows. Chewing, laughing, pulling faces. Nurses attend to each head, massaging peanut butter on the scalps and running cafeteria forks through the hair in search of nits. The mother next to me is whispering, promising God she'll be better—she'll be the fucking Virgin Mary, just not this, Lord—but I know better than to pray for a B-side catastrophe.

At dinner, my daughter twirls Cup-O-Noodles around her fork. I can't stop staring at her headless head. Before the outbreak she always looked like a broomstick with a melon on top, but now she's just a broomstick. It's a weird improvement, I tell her. She raises the fork to where her mouth should be and noodles spill on the floor. This happens over and over. But for once there's no eye-rolling when I call her Princess, no sighs when I launch my nightly egg at the neighbor blasting his music. Princess just stands on the lawn holding an empty dog leash.

The next day she bangs loudly on the door until my ex appears and hugs her gently as she races past him up the stairs.

It's not my fault, I tell him. It never is, he sighs.

Now that she's headless, Princess doesn't want me to take her back to church. On Sundays she'd rather go to the park and play hide-and-go-seek with the other headless children. They turn in jagged circles, like broken carousel horses. But I still catch her kneeling beside her bed. Is she pleading for the return of her lost head? Or offering gratitude that it's gone? When I was a girl, I thought God would be my crawlspace, but now I understand he created us so we could be his.

Sometimes the school sends progress reports on the heads. *Your child is a genius*, the letter says. I read it to the other girls between sets until the ink is smudged with glitter. Before the outbreak, the principal always said in a few years we'd be doing a mother-daughter routine, but now, apparently, Princess's head does complex math equations and recites Emily Dickinson's poetry.

You're amazing, Princess, I tell her, but remember rich guys don't care about who painted the Eiffel Tower. Just if you'll do anal. Her broomstick body rocks back and forth on the stairs.

The headless girls have a sleepover. I sip fireballs, show them how to fake a pregnancy for alimony, and when to use an Oxford comma. I'm not sure there's more to life than this, I tell the girls, but they're too busy feeling petals, feathers, marshmallows. All the soft things they can get their hands on. I give them each a tampon soaked in Tanqueray. They keep coming back for more until they slump against the walls. In the morning, one of the Mormon mothers threatens to sue me for child endangerment. I give her the box of tampons and what's left of the Hennessy. You need this more than I do, I say.

It's a weird place, this Utah. Full of L.A. transplants who swear they'll never go back, and L.A. dreamers desperate to get out of here. There's a different story for everyone under all this sand. Just a shame it swallows you up when you start digging for it. The Mormons are nice. I've had four baptisms. They look at me and sneer. But I was born here. I'm salt folk. Lick me, grind me, melt me—I just brine back. From salt I came and to salt I'll return, I tell these wannabe believers. Until then I got no home. Just a mutiny of gray pubes.

How long will the heads be quarantined? I ask the school office. Nobody knows. Nobody tells us anything. In fairy tales time is a hiccup if it exists at all, but in the suburbs you feel it like a virus replicating invisibly inside you. The other mothers are frantic, desperate for their girls to get their heads so they can go back to cheerleading and bulimia. Am I a bad mother if I don't want the old Princess back? Lately, she's like the daughter I always wanted, helping me pee in my ex's gas tank and while I pretend to slip at the Gas-N-Go she swipes a pack of cigarettes and Slim Jims. In the alley I smoke until my insides charcoal and tell her having a cunt is like a map of Russia full of weird forests and bears and the more you wander around the more likely you'll turn into a witch.

Just think, if it wasn't for the lice you'd be rehearsing for the fair right now, I tell her as we put laxatives in the auto shop coffee machine. I don't know why they call it a fair. There's no deep-fried Oreos and no getting finger-banged by Heber P. Talbot on the Ferris Wheel. Just a bunch of over achievers standing in front of cheap poster boards talking about history. South African Apartheid. Martin Luther and the Protestant Reformation. Harriet Tubman. The Cold War. The Jackson 5 and the birth of hip-hop. Everyone gets a tragedy. Why don't they talk about the school playground with the radioactive geese? Or the quarterback turned bishop who resurrected twice? We've had four murderers in this town. World-class killers. Last year, Princess had the Mountain Meadows massacre. The Mormons are nice, of course. It's just that everybody loves the Holocaust.

Yesterday, I tried to convince her to fill the library toilets with goldfish, but Princess would rather be with her headless girlfriends. They ride the bus all over town, leaning close to strangers with their headless stumps. They call themselves the Snow Whites. They say you can feel it when they kiss you and then your life is never the same. Last week a kissed man lactated honey. And the waitress hoping to go to Hollywood coughed up her own stomach. And the man who fell down the elevator shaft had winning lotto tickets in his pocket. People think it's a trick. If it were a boy with syphilis or a girl with acid splashed on her face they'd call it a miracle. But a kiss from a headless girl is too much.

When Princess was little, she kept a pet turtle in a shoebox. Said one day it just appeared. Like magic. Wouldn't let anyone else see it, but for a nickel the other kids could stick their finger in a hole she'd cut out and feel it. One girl with orange hair like a firebird came to see the turtle every day. When she ran out of nickels, Princess let her pay with kisses. Then one day the girl left crying and said what Princess did was a dirty trick. Empty all this time, I heard her say, like she had no idea life is cruel and sometimes we're cruel with it.

The Zitmeister stares at me. I breathe for the first time in what feels like hours. *Blink once if you're okay, twice if you're in trouble*, he says. I lower the lipstick detonator and as he hands over the bag of fry sauce I can see he's thrown in a handful of fries. They smell like greasy heaven. *Freedom fries*, the Zitmeister says. *Eat your fucking heart out.*

The bus takes me in loops. The sirens get loud then wane. The billboard says I can sign up for truck driving classes at the community college. Or maybe I'll be one of those nurses who collects blood. I like the look of blood. Maybe I'll sail to the Virgin Islands and recycle my virginity. Who am I kidding? All I want is a kiss from the Snow Whites. One of them is walking up and down the aisle, arms hung limp at her side. I reach out and take her hand and she leans a headless head against my shoulder. Her chest goes in and out with these lonely breaths. Cheer up, baby. It's a disaster. But at least it's ours. I reach out and comb the emptiness of where her head should be. Have I told you how pretty your face is? It's a weird improvement. I wonder if she can hear me. I wonder if I am the turtle or the shoebox.

We'll take this bus to the end of the line. Run barefoot into the Salt Lake and float until we're fleshy margaritas. Dive into sickly green water. Come up for air. Throat on fire. Wasps dancing inside my eyes. The headless girl waves for me to follow her. Behind us the glow of that white temple floating at the base of the mountains, calling us in from the dark to heavens unknown. We swim deeper. Then sit on the sandbar and chew freedom fries until the pulp is a cloud in my mouth. Soft, but never soft enough.

The Sprites of Panguitch

After the train derailed and all the chemicals spilled, the mayor outlawed death but nobody believed him. There was a press conference. No more room in the cemetery, he told us. We can't rezone land and the city council is in recess. Death is now on holiday. Don't be afraid to live, he smiled.

What could we do? He was the mayor. The law is the law.

Nobody thought it was a big deal until two days later mama found the chickens screeching in the coop. I had seen her butcher them the night before: wring the necks and pop the heads until the blood made a hot syrup in the dust. But here they were, walking around like Lazarus.

A few of the neighbors came to see the resurrected chickens. They were the same people who went to see the Yeti in the retirement home get baptized in Kanab, and visited the girl in Provo who ate a potato chip shaped like the Virgin Mary and got pregnant. They asked mama all kinds of questions: if a camel can pass through the eye of a needle before a rich man, then how many devils fit inside a rain drop? Was it the city of Enoch that had come to Vernal or just UFOs? How many handshakes does it take to ascend to the ninth heaven?

Mama said this was no time to get religious. It was just stubborn chickens.

She cut off one of the chickens' heads so everyone could see. We gathered around it and waited. There was a mess of blood. Nothing happened. People got bored and left.

"It would be something to see a miracle," I said that night as we ate supper. "Probably just wild chickens sneaking into the coop." I was quiet before saying the next part. "Or maybe you didn't actually kill them. Daddy always said you were no good with your hands."

Mama said I didn't understand. She said words have a strange magic.

———

After the parade, they took sick people from the hospital and drove them in buses outside the town limits. They had tubes in their noses and needles in their arms and you could see their underwear through a flap in the back, but none of that mattered anymore. Death had been outlawed. Why did we need a hospital? We shipped them off like postcards in the mail.

Not long after they wrapped the hospital in yellow tape, a few of the bodies they had driven out of town came back with tubes in their noses and needles in their arms but not one of them was wearing underwear. They were soaking wet and mad as hell. Skip Vanderhousen, Delia Burgos, and the old lady that rang the chapel bells. There were a dozen others. They said they weren't dead. They said they had the memory of elephants. They yelled with voices angry as a train whistle. A few of them had wanted to die but it just didn't happen. Let us die with dignity, they begged.

The mayor apologized. The law was the law.

Well, what the hell do we do now? they wanted to know.

Nobody had an answer. We knew it was unwise to negotiate with the nearly deads.

The mayor and his staff told them they could stay here in limbo or find another hospital in the next county. The dead said they didn't want limbo. They wanted the paradise they had been promised.

Go to hell, the mayor said.

With the hospital shut down, nature was left to its own devices. Cuts and broken bones were left to mend on their own. Sicknesses came and went like the breeze. Pretty soon people forgot how to die. They grew old, took to their beds, broke their watches, said goodbyes, and waited. They made their own certificates selecting cause of death: suicide, starvation, acute thrombosis of the heart, aneurysm. They stared for hours at those certificates. Imagining. Waiting. When nothing happened, they put on their clothes, went back to old jobs and their begrudged lives.

It wasn't fair. Daddy died months ago. Now the cemetery was all chained up. At night I hopped the gate and stood over his grave. I told him death was illegal. I told him he could come back. I kept waiting to see him at the door one morning all gray and greasy and missing his underwear, but it was like he decided not to come home. He wasn't the best of men, but he was all we had. How could he leave us like this?

I thought it over on the roof. When daddy was still alive that's where I used to watch for him coming home from the alfalfa fields. It's where we used to take the scrap metal to add to the antenna we were building. Daddy said he was going to teach me science and we would catch lightning in a bottle. It's a law of attraction, he said. We had a pretty big antenna but never caught any lightning.

When the mayor outlawed death, I scrounged the junk-yard, but I wasn't sure what kind of antenna would attract dead fathers. Mama used to stick her head out of the window late at night and yell, "Five more minutes up there. You can catch lightning, just don't catch yourself on fire."

I stared at the alfalfa fields. The mayor said this town was paradise. Mama said living is a nightmare and everyone is doing their best to wake up.

———

It took a month before people went funny with the idea of living forever. Women quit having babies. The chickens stopped laying eggs. Then the animals went missing. Frankie Allen lost his dog. We stopped hearing coyotes howl and there was no more cicada music in the trees. There were no fish in the ponds, no birds in the sky. Stars seemed to shine less and less until we never saw the stars. Everything was mist. It drifted on us like a parched tongue. The earth cracked and getting close to sinkholes we smelled sulfur and old cereal. What was happening to us? People shrugged. Roads buzzed with heat. What wasn't desert became muck and the rest fizzled into an eerie gray weirdness.

Mama gave me a pixie cut. I watched the wind carry away my hair.

Factories closed. Shops empty. People gone. They put everything they could fit in the back of a truck and drove off. Death was outlawed but all around us was death: the death of roads, buildings, houses. All the things we had created. Those were the laws of attraction now.

I told Frankie I would stay and wait for his dog to come back.

"You're a fucking loon," he said and walked off.

At church, the bishop said this was just the beginning. He said this was a reverse creationism.

"What happens at the end of a reverse creationism?" we wanted to know.

"Is *ex nihilo* eternal?"

"When do we get to create God in our image?"

The bishop said he didn't have answers. He was just the messenger. He said there was no stopping it. The sin was inside each of us, and God was sweeping under the rug the mess we had made.

———

In July, the town became a loony-bin. People marched outside the mayor's mansion. As a joke, they dressed up in animal skins like a bunch of idiots. They were dogs, cats, jackals, vultures, rodents, and even a water buffalo. All the animals we had lost. They wandered the roads, a perverse reincarnation. They didn't answer to their names. They squawked, growled, crawled, and flapped in the dust. It was truly asinine.

"This land is sick," mama said. "Used to swallow everything we fed it. Now we feed it poison and expect rainbows in return. God help us."

"If I could be any animal," I told mama, "I'd be an elephant. They never forget a thing."

"Careful, girl. Maybe you'll grow up and want to forget," mama said.

One day we were out watching the riots when a man dressed in donkey skin grabbed mama and asked if she was a virgin named Mary. Mama chased him off with her purse.

She didn't want me going out by myself anymore—too dangerous, she said—but I went to the junkyard anyway. I couldn't quit the antenna. I couldn't quit daddy. He was out there somewhere. Maybe dying had wiped his memory. Maybe he was one of them now. A snake or an armadillo. It didn't matter to me. If I caught the lightning he would find his way home.

"Your father's gone. You know that, right?" mama said one night tucking me into bed.

"I know," I said, but we both knew it was a lie. The dead don't die. They're always with you.

Then one night I was coming back from the junkyard with a piece of tin almost as big as me when I passed the mayor's mansion and saw the people dressed like animals loaded into vans. The sheriff and his men were pulling off the costumes and tossing them into barrels which were set on fire. Some went quietly but others screamed when their costumes were pulled away, as if they really were skins, as if they really believed they could escape all this by becoming animals.

The next morning, I looked in the barrels at a mess of feathers and fur. There was blood on the sidewalk. I ran fingers through my hair. I asked mama if they were taking them to the zoo or a wildlife sanctuary and she said this is what happens when creation goes in reverse and everybody forgets what it's like to be a decent person.

The thunderstorms came in August. Sky crackling and humming. I waited on the roof but never caught lightning in a bottle. There was still no sign of daddy. Mama reminded me I could catch all the lightning I wanted but not to catch on fire.

Mama was of two minds about fire. She didn't want me to catch lightning, but she was keen to burn anything she could get her hands on. She'd disappear into the attic and come out with boxes of photos or old furniture and we'd make a real blaze. "Smoke signals," she'd say. Like how the Paiutes used to talk with each other after the Mormons stole all their land. "It used to be a prayer was enough to talk to God," mama said, "but now he's gone AWOL, and we have to burn things to get his attention." We'd watch the smoke and when the storm came, she'd lean back in her chair and say the sky sure is pretty when it's sick.

Mama liked thunder and lightning. She liked to watch the sky for red sprites. She explained it to me the way daddy had explained it to her. She said any fool can see the blue jets. There. See? Those blue spurts? That's just sad lightning. But the red sprites are tricky.

"They're high up in the clouds. Hiding. Shy things. Like pixies. A little afraid. Flashes of red tentacles like jellyfish in a ballet. You've got to blink to see them, baby. Don't be afraid if you do. It's calling you. Don't be afraid if it stretches out its tentacles. It just wants to say hello."

Each night we watched the sky and mama dipped her finger in perfume to rub all over her neck. It gave me a headache. She never told me, but I think it was to keep the men from coming around the house. After daddy died there were plenty of men, like moths to the flame. They said these were dangerous times and women shouldn't be alone in big empty houses surrounded by alfalfa. Mama told them she grew up on a farm and knew how to castrate a bull. The men laughed but they didn't believe her, not even when she dipped her finger in perfume and set it on fire, waving it in circles until the flame disappeared. The men called her a trick.

"Are you a trick, mama?"

"I don't know what I am," she said and stared into the clouds with one hand on her chest.

I'd always known there was an issue with mama's heart. That's what daddy used to say when we were on the roof together.

"Let's stay here a while longer and not bother her right now," he would say. "She's got an issue."

I'd heard stories at school that a woman's issue could cause all the blood to slip from you, like opening up a window and letting out all the warm air. I decided that's what happened to this town. Without the heart there is no blood and without the blood there is no death and without the death it's all just nonsense.

More and more I saw mama sleeping at the foot of the bed in the middle of the night and I could tell she was having an issue, but almost like she was trying to pass it on to me, like she wanted me to be her sprite in the night.

The days went on. I felt heavier. That's when I knew she'd somehow leached her issue onto me. I wanted it out of me so I wouldn't become a trick like mama. I closed my eyes in bed and waited for the dark to fill the room. When it was dark dark, I opened the blinds and let the moon spill in. I tried to walk up the moonlight like a staircase hoping I could leave all my issues behind.

But I was too heavy.

Then one morning the sheets were wet and sticky with blood. It left a smear on my hand almost like chocolate, not bright like the thunderstorm sprites in the sky.

Mama knocked on the bathroom door. "What's going on in there?" she said.

"Nothing," I said quietly, "I got an issue, that's all."

———————————

Mama's perfume did nothing to scare away the rooster-man. He must have fooled the sheriff and gone into hiding after the last of the animal people were taken away. We saw him come out of the trees one morning, scurry across the road, grab something in a ditch, then hurry back to the woods. For a few days he sat on the fence just watching the house. Mama went and gave him a glass of sarsaparilla then shooed him away with the broom.

He was back the next morning. Then before long he was eating supper with us. It was hard to see if he was wearing a costume or if the feathers had been tarred to him or if they were just tangled wads of hair. His face was pock-marked. He had bushy tufts of hair with crusted mud and was so skinny and worn away by the sun he looked like a scarecrow. I believed he was a rooster-man, but mama said he was just ugly.

He didn't say much. He didn't do any of the things a rooster is supposed to do. He never crowed. He never preened. He drank the whisky daddy kept in the cabinet. He refused to sleep in the coop and instead locked himself with mama inside the bedroom and laughed and laughed.

The only thing he knew how to do was fight. Before he liked to play cards but lost a few teeth gambling and turned to fights.

"Fists are easier than flushes," he said in a kind of slurred and chirpy voice.

He had no job, no house, and no family left to speak of him. Otherwise, he was a perfect gentleman.

One morning a few of his friends showed up and they cleared out the barn. That night there was a bareknuckle brawl. Mama said I couldn't watch but I crept inside without anybody seeing and stayed up in the rafters out of sight. There was a lot of hooting. People passed money and bottles of whisky back and forth. They made a ring out of hay bundles. The two fighters tied themselves together at the wrist with some rope. Then they fought. They scratched, wrestled, kicked, clawed, and gouged each other. There was blood everywhere. One man wasn't moving. He looked dead. The voices got louder, and everything seemed to blur. One of the fighters breathed into the dead man's mouth and punched his chest with a fist. Bubbles formed on the dead man's lips. He turned over and vomited. Then he got back on his feet.

"Again," the dead man said.

The crowd cheered. I couldn't decide what was living or dead or if there was any difference.

The next morning the rooster-man was all beat up, hacking up blood in the sink and blowing bloody snot rockets out of his nose. He pulled out a tooth and flicked it in my cereal bowl. Mama was asleep in the other room. It was raining. There was no food in the house. The rooster-man's friends had eaten it all. The rooster-man put on clothes, and we walked to the store for milk and eggs.

"How old are you?" he said.

"Eleven."

"Can you fight?"

"No."

"Have you ever had a wet dick?"

"What's a dick?"

He sighed and mussed my pixie hair. "Well, then you're not eleven yet."

He mumbled the rest of the way, but I didn't understand a word of it.

On the walk home, he opened the carton of milk, took one chug, and was mad as hell that it had spoiled. He tossed the carton but didn't aim well or wasn't looking because it landed on a group of boys sitting on the curb.

The rooster-man took one look at those boys and ran. For a rooster he ran pretty damn fast and a few times I believed he might actually take flight. I ran too but wasn't fast enough. When I came back to the house, bloody and bruised and half-naked sopping wet with rage, mama's bedroom door was locked. I could hear them on the other side, grunting like animals.

I went up on the roof. It was still raining. There was no lightning. Mama stuck her head out the window. "You're still up here? Go to the store and get some milk and eggs. Go on. You can catch lightning some other time."

I put my hand on the antenna and waited for this whole mess to catch fire.

———————

It didn't take long for the sheriff to find the rooster-man. One night he was in the barn drinking whisky and the next morning the sheriff found him already handcuffed and half-naked in mama's bed. Mama made a scene. She was crying and laughing all at once. Then she was slapping and biting and had to be handcuffed until they drove the rooster-man away. Mama blinked furiously as she looked at the sky. She was pale, like the blood had been vampired from her.

She slept in the coop that night, probably hoping for her own reverse creationism. I found her the next morning. It was thunder storming again. The sky pixied with sound and color.

I watched the eggs crack open and little chicklets stumble out. Half of them died after taking a few breaths. I watched the hens eat their dead babies, as if they believed the dead could save the living.

I helped mama out of the coop and into a bath. I washed her hair. I helped her into her clean clothes and told her we could go to the store for milk and eggs. She pretended to listen to me, bathing herself in that god-awful bottle of perfume until she was a greasy mess.

She lit a cigarette.

A sudden flash of blue filled the room, like lightning had spit from somewhere deep inside mama. Then a whoosh. It knocked me against the door. When I got to my feet everything was a blur. Then I saw her halfway down the road. She ran in twisted circles like the devil's mistress, sometimes fast and other times so slow it was almost like she was moving in reverse, not a sound from her—just some old bird waving her arms as if trying to catch flight.

On rainy days when I close my eyes, I rewind the memory over and over and can still see her: a swirl of yellow and orange leaping through the dark sweeps of alfalfa, a smoke signal to a blind God carried away in some strange laws of attraction.

A Whale

The woman walks through the dust, dragging behind her the whale. She is small and lithe, her skin kissed by the sun. The whale is fifty tons of melancholy. It moans what may be a lullaby or an apology. People crowd into the town square. The woman rubs the whale's flank and it sings. She tells the people it is her father.

See the eyes? she says, a daughter knows.

Feeling tricked, the townspeople leave disappointed.

Come, the woman whispers to the whale as she knots the rope to its tail. The ocean is not that far.

At night, the woman and the whale rest. She pours buckets of water over the whale's skin.

She scrapes off barnacles, polishes its baleen. Carrying the whale has made her heavy, as if something has breached inside her, slowly turning her to stone.

In the next town, the woman lies and says the whale is not her father but a prehistoric monster. In the town after, she tells them he is the constellation Cetus fallen from the sky. Once she convinced them it was one of Wickham's whales, imported from Australia for an experimental breeding farm in the Great Salt Lake, only to escape over a century ago. The people come a second, then a third time. They fill her purse with coins. She wonders why lies, that strange species of alphabet, feel like angel wings, but the truth is a heavy stone.

At night, she reads to the whale from a children's book. *The No-Nos.* A tale of disobedient girls who say *no! no! no!* until their faces twist into gruesome shapes. She holds the pictures close to the whale eye as if trying to make it remember something. It blinks slowly.

The ocean is not that far, the woman tells the whale.

The woman does not sleep because she knows she will dream of how after the sun bore down and the seas dried up she found the whale trapped in an empty canal downtown where a nearby sign said ELEVATION 4,265. Night after night she went to it. Crusted in salt, the whale sang its low, languid tones. She does not sleep because she fears the whale will steal her dreams and then what will be hers to remember? The woman does not let the whale sleep either.

They keep walking. She clings to faith that simmers in her heart like blubber. The ocean is not that far, she tells the whale. The rope frays, then snaps. The woman borrows a farmer's bale hook, hooks the whale in the flukes, and resumes her dragging. They walk through salt flats. The sun rises, sets. The whale sings. The woman's back aches. Her feet bleed. She doesn't know how much longer she can keep doing this. They keep walking.

That night, in the dark, the woman touches her own body, committing the dimples and curves and distances between limbs to memory. She leans against the whale's flank and listens. A whale's heart is an idle, hollow thing.

The next night, a mother and her children find the woman pouring water over the whale.

The mother stands barefoot with the three little blonde girls beside her and another swaddled in the crook of her elbow.

Show's over, the woman tells them. The mother stares at the whale, unblinking. Is he really your father? she asks. The teeth of her half-smile are like little mildewed tombstones. She pulls the bundle of rags close to her chest. Do his dreams really heal? she asks.

Earlier, the woman had offered to sell the townspeople the whale's dreams as a tonic, but the townspeople had only murmured. Women who carry whales are not to be trusted.

Please, the mother says, my little one.

The woman suspects the mother is not superstitious, does not believe a whale's dreams can cure the child's sickness. She wants only a distraction from watching her baby die.

Using a dull blade, the woman flenses the whale's flank and removes a fistful of blubber. The whale moans. The woman flenses deeper, feeling an unspeakable pleasure. She simmers the blubber in a vat, and the oil rises to the surface. The little blonde girls lick their lips. The mother shakes a few coins from her purse.

No, no, the woman says.

She watches as the mother and her children suck the dream oil off their fingers. She watches as the mother and her children grow smaller and smaller in the distance.

The woman reaches inside the blubbery whale. It moans. The wound is deep. It pulses. It will heal. Like it always does. Like a dream, waiting to open all over again.

The ocean is not far, the woman tells the whale.

The whale sings a lullaby, unaware that tomorrow they will turn inland, that ahead there is a constellation of towns.

Go Wrong with You

Bareknuckle brawl on the Virgin. We bite, we scratch, we slap like two ballerinas. He kicks my ribs until it sounds like gospel music. Under different circumstances I might have taken this beating only to surprise him later by slashing his tires and pissing in his gas tank. Instead, the man gives me a bloody baptism. It's his lucky day. Every man has a few.

My eye is almost swollen shut, but I can see the woman and kid gathering up their picnic in a hurry. They look like they could be my wife and daughter, only their faces are dreamlike.

I shouldn't be on the river. I should have listened to the cards. I don't think of myself as a cursed man. Just unlucky with living.

My wife didn't believe in the cards. She listened to public radio broadcasts and wept over missing children reports. I told her it was all in the cards. She warned me not to believe. Because when you start to believe what the cards tell you, well, then you're finished.

It's over. Nothing on the Virgin but me. It's quiet. The sun is doing what sun does. My head feels full of maple syrup, but the pain reminds me I am still breathing.

Wash off the blood. Look for a cigarette. Keep moving. The cards say always keep moving.

The trail is unclear. They've headed downstream. No, they've run into the trees. No, they're notifying authorities. Fuck. I should have listened to the cards and bought a GPS.

I take inventory. Winston—my pet snake, my comrade— is unscathed. He's a little twitchy from the fight and tries to swallow his own tail. I'm not sure what you feed a three-month old boa.

In the canoe we got firecrackers. We got duct tape. We got jerky, binoculars, extra underwear. We got my baseball bat, the one that hit three homeruns in the Kansas City amateur baseball league. Then I see the hole in the bottom of the canoe and all the beer cans empty. This is a problem.

It hurts to stand longer than eight seconds. I feel the cuts, the scratches, the bruises. They'll fade. They always do. But for now they sing.

"Hey, Winston." He ignores me. He's got a good swallow on his tail. "Hey, goddamn it. Did you see which way they went?" I try and pry his mouth open, but his jaws are clenched. He's too young to know any better.

My rescue has gone to hell. Okay, it wasn't exactly a rescue. All I wanted was to see my daughter and give her the inheritance. Winston. I rescued him from the local pet store when nobody was looking. Most fathers would bring a tiara or some cheap-ass plastic doll to a family reunion. Fuck that. Every little girl needs a pet to call their best friend.

The cards say she's here on the Virgin River. But the cards also say I'm cursed. What else can a cursed man do but commit himself to the ridiculous? I have committed myself to a father's love. Wasn't it Willie Nelson, the only good Willie, who sang only love can ruin a curse?

———————

Big Frida finds me curled up in the busted canoe. I smell like a dead fish. She slaps me twice.

"Stupid-ass marshmallow. You're bleeding," she says. She has frizzy tufts of hair shooting out from under her beret with the gilded letters. *Fuck the Police*. She's got hands that can strangle a hog no problem.

"I got more blood," I mumble.

She slaps me again. For such a small woman with a ridiculous name she slaps hard.

"You been telling people on the river about me?"

"Nobody on the river but me," I lie.

"Yeah, and you're just chasing ghosts."

That's the problem with coming out West. Everything goes extinct except the ghosts in your head. People here believe the craziest shit. Like old Bob Lindquist who still pans for gold down in Flaming Gorge. Like the Mormons who think they're all white and radiant because they stand on the right hand of God, but really it's just the uranium in their water. Still, I'd rather have a wild country than a sane one. Where there's wildness there's hope.

"Come on, stupid-ass marshmallow," she says, "I'll clean you up. Again."

There are two things Big Frida likes: a man with an appetite, and a man in misery. She's lucky to have me.

We walk slowly along the riverbank that cuts through the canyon. On the other side of these cliffs is Zion, a place for those of one heart and one mind, but over here is no man's land. Half a mile upstream is Big Frida's BBQ shack just off the highway. The place smells like sweat and barbeque sauce with just a hint of chicken shit. Elmore James is making a guitar weep on the jukebox. *You say you hurting, you almost lost your mind. The girl you love, she hurts you all the time.* I'm the only customer. I'm always the only customer.

Big Frida washes the mud and vomit from my hair. Hands me a cigarette, feeds me brisket that melts in my mouth. She gives me beer until I feel so heavy I can't move off the stool. Winston curls inside a bucket under the bar. Big Frida is terrified of snakes.

"Bleeding too much is bad for your health," Big Frida says.

"You should see the other guy," I laugh.

Big Frida shakes her head. "You go looking for trouble and a wolf is going to mess up your shit."

"I'm cursed."

"You're not cursed," Big Frida says. "Just a marshmallow."

I've read the books and spoken with the elders. I know the history of curses. Inverted Pelvis. Mexican Blood Wedding. Bamboo Teeth. The list goes on and on. But nobody has a name for mine.

The cards say my curse will be lifted on the Virgin. What that means is anybody's guess. I do what the cards demand, saint or sin, even if it is unpopular with my brain. Even if the cards tell you to get a room at the Virgin River Motel with a girl who you only find out later is not of legal age and gets you arrested for pervading the innocence of the state, even then you listen to the cards because sooner or later they will lead you to where you need to be. I believe this. I have to. I have no choice but to wander the Virgin. There is a poetry here. Water ripples into ripples and reminds us that nothing stays the same forever and all things must eventually erode downstream.

Or I'm misreading the cards and I am not well. Years ago, I heard a man on the television say we have to be afraid of the known unknowns. But what do you do when your life is just one unknown unknown after the other? Perhaps I am cursed. Perhaps I am fortunate. It's difficult to tell the difference.

———

"Come on, marshmallow. Start talking," Big Frida says.

"I'm all out of confessions."

Our relationship is simple. For a plate of barbeque and all the beer I can drink, I tell Big Frida my life story. It can be anything as long as it is true. With the Virgin drying up the fishermen and bird peepers don't come like they used to which means I'm the only victim of Big Frida's magic.

It's a fragile house of cards we're playing with. Can't say I mind pimping my past with the hope of finding my future. I'm running out of true stories, but she seems to have an endless supply of beer. She's a soul eater, Big Frida is.

"My wife used to fart in the shower," I say. "Towards the end, when I knew we were finished, I used to wait outside the door and listen."

"You told me that last month," Big Frida says. "Try again."

"Can't you just read me the cards?"

Big Frida locks the door. She cranks up the jukebox and straddles me. She bites my neck. I bite back.

"Oooo," she says. "The marshmallow is a cougar. I like that. Say it. Say, *I'm a cougar.*"

I sigh. "I'm a cougar."

She pulls up her dress and puts my hand on her old butt cheek. I can see the backside of her in the mirror across the room. Damn. That's an old butt cheek. "No," I mumble, "I can't cheat on the Virgin."

We're two cursed things, me and the Virgin. Trout won't spawn. Trees always on fire. Hot. Cold. Wet. Dry. She can't make up her mind. She's less a river than a dusty tongue now. Fifty years of farmers stealing her soul and city councils selling her off to hotels who drain her so rich old man can pop blue pills and soak in hot tubs after a round of golf. When I'm not hunting Vikings, I bring her buckets of water everyday but maybe you can't save a cursed thing.

"She's gone," Big Frida whispers.

"No. She's not gone yet."

"You hear me, marshmallow man?" she says, tapping a bony finger against my forehead. "There anything left in there?"

Big Frida is a rotten sight naked. She is small and wrinkled and I wonder how a stiff breeze hasn't blown her into a dark talcum powder. It's gross, but I don't let go. She doesn't let go. What else can you do on the Virgin? She clenches me between her thighs, and we rock back and forth, and Elmore keeps killing that guitar. Or maybe it's killing him.

My friend, let's call him Irish, lost his wife to Baptists in Tulsa. One day she started reading the Lord's word, and then eighty-seven hours later she stood up and said, "I need to be saved." Irish said, "It's been a pleasure." Then she walked out. Now she's lost. That's what he says, anyway. But I've been in his apartment and seen the cans of Schwengers in every corner and the wedding dress on the floor and her old makeup she left in the cabinet and the television always on mute and poor stupid Irish always looking at the tattoo on his arm that says *Rota Taro Orat Tora Ator*. There is only one lost thing in that man's world.

I've notified him of the moral of his story: Do not bite the hand that feeds you, because the hand you bite may be your own.

I am not so pathetic as my so-called friend Irish. I am not lost. I follow the cards. When my wife wandered off, as I told the neighbors, I went looking for her. I was determined. I found her with this southern type, a real Civil War buff, the kind of guy who slept with knives under his pillow and stockpiled gunpowder in his cabinets. Then one night my roof blew up and the next day I was served divorce papers. I couldn't prove anything, but how many other acquaintances did I have with access to explosives? When I tried to tell my wife the kind of crazy she was dealing with she said I was sabotaging her love life.

"I am the love of your life," I told her.

"No," she said, "you and me are a maelstrom of difficulty."

Nine years married and now the roof was blown sky-high and all I had to show for our holy matrimony were a few Styx albums and a scorching case of hemorrhoids.

Maelstrom? No shit.

I tried to throw it back in her face and take my daughter away from her but what can I say, Irish is a shitty lawyer.

Big Frida fans the cards over the table. Pick three, she says, but I pick four. Ten of Pentacles. The Tower. The Empress. The Hanged Man. Two love cards. Two chaos cards.

What does it mean?

"You're fucked," she says.

But we both already knew that.

It happens every day. I've told Big Frida this a hundred times and every time she says, "Oh, you sad fucking marshmallow," but I tell her again how you take a child to the park with enough bread to give the ducks acid reflux and you run in the grass and between games of hide-and-go-seek she is like ripples in water, there one minute and gone the next, and the other parents say they saw her get in the car with a blond man big as a Viking, with weird tattoos even, and you scream and beg that this isn't your life and convince yourself you never had a child. A child? No, that was the miscarried child you just lost, yes, how silly of you to forget your wife miscarried four years ago and the child, now the missing child, never existed, so she couldn't have been stolen by Vikings, and what a relief that illusion brings if only for an hour, because you know what's true, maybe, if only this isn't you with your heart twisted and maybe if you retrace your steps she might suddenly reappear and you won't have to go on the evening news and cry how a Viking stole your child, how you are a victim of chance, a natural fool of fortune, hell, not chance but fate, hell, not fate but a curse and then you start looking at every face at the playground, at the school, at the bus stop knowing that if you stare at enough children you might just see her within the others, your baby girl, you might just get lucky because you don't want to move on, you don't want the pain to end, you want the emptiness to swell with sadness and fear and flood and burst, just like that, because the only true thing is that you never want to heal.

"Lost things are often found," Irish told me after the police said there's no such thing as Vikings anymore. "Just not in the place you expect them."

What a piece of shit.

I can't help but believe that all of this is like the dream I keep having: I am a sperm swimming up the birth canal and fighting off the others with my slingshot tail, asphyxiating my brothers and sisters, a microscopic act of genocide as I swim my way through the mob with their little mouths wriggling and laughing, saying, *Isn't this warm? Isn't this so much nicer than before?* But I'm too late, and someone else atombombs the egg, and the rest of us just slowly disintegrate.

Big Frida says I'm not well, but the cards haven't told me what I am.

———

After they called our daughter a cold case my wife told me I was cursed. She found another husband. Then she came out West. I asked Irish what to do and he told me the answer is in the cards. So, I closed my eyes and put my finger on the map and woke up on the Virgin.

———

Big Frida watches from the car as I roll the steel drum down the embankment. Water I stole from the reservoir that feeds a retirement community. I tell Big Frida I'm just trying to fix what went wrong. "Oh, marshmallow. There's no fixing sadness. You're just her landlord," Big Frida says. "But don't worry. She'll come pay the rent every day."

If the cards have taught me anything it's you can empty yourself into anything. Drugs, women, God. Pick your poison. That's the only way to heal. I pour the last of the fifty-gallon drum into the river. Water spills slowly over the rocks and trickles downstream. Tomorrow I'll pour another fifty-gallon drum. And the day after that, and the day after that. It's not much. But it's something.

Being on the Virgin seems like a dream. I'm half in the water and half on the riverbank like a dumb tetrapod. The sun is going down. Burnt trees loom over the river like watchtowers. I've climbed into those trees before and stayed up all night watching it go from dusk to midnight to orange to clueless before it all settles into haze. You can see south to the old uranium mine. Supposedly, they dug too deep and now the yellowcake is in the water and that's why the Virgin is drying up. I went to see it for myself last year. Crawled down the shaft expecting to find neon caves like an alien nightclub. But it was just dark tunnels. Vein after vein of silence. And since then, this haze choking my eyes.

Big Frida read the cards a second time but there was nothing new. She showed me the Lovers and the Fool. Which was I? What was at the end of the river? Not even Big Frida could say. So, I came downstream to wander like a ghost.

And then I see her.

I'd followed the markings in the mud and the runes on the trees like a fool and the cards don't lie. She's right there, my lost baby girl. What are the chances? She doesn't look like the baby girl I remember. Her hair is different. But there she is on the sandbar watching the sky turn indigo.

I wave. She waves back.

"Is that your snake?" she says.

I pull Winston off my neck. "I brought him for you."

"For me?"

"You love animals, don't you?"

"That's a big snake."

"He can swallow you whole."

"Not me," she says stubbornly.

"His name is Winston. He's your inheritance."

I reach into my pocket and pull out a bag of soggy marsh-mallows. Her face scrunches up. "We can roast these later. Like I promised. Remember?"

"I need to pee," she says all of a sudden. She does the little pee dance. It just about breaks my heart that somebody left this poor girl all alone with nobody to help her pee.

"Where's mom?" I ask.

My baby girl points to the trees on the other side of the river.

"Come on," I say. "Let's pee."

I turn my back and get a good stream going. Baby girl seems confused.

"It's okay," I say. "You can pee standing up."

She pisses all over her legs. She finds it hilarious. I pull off my shirt and wipe her clean. Then I brush the hair out of her face and pin it back like it had been in the picture of us before I smashed the glass. I kiss her on the cheek. I can feel her trembling.

It's like she doesn't remember me. Daughters are tricky like that. Sons just want to kill you, but daughters will mess with your head and turn your heart inside out. Every man with a daughter should do community theatre. Do all your fuck ups on stage. I was Lear once. *I am the natural fool of Fortune. I am cut to th' brains. Come, come, I am a king, a man of salt.* I've been Learing ever since. Hard to take off a costume that fits.

We walk back to the sandbar. I look through the bags. There are no maps of Scandinavia, no reindeer jerky, no prayer books to Odin. There are towels and booze and books my wife would never read. It's strange.

"Where does mom keep her cigarettes?"

"She doesn't smoke."

"She always smokes," I say.

"My dad says he doesn't understand why he can't smoke in his office."

"What does your dad do?"

"He's a teacher."

"Probably a tenured professor of assholes."

"My dad says we're not to take the name of God in vain."

"Don't call him dad. I'm your dad."

"You're not my dad," she says and takes a few steps back.

Just then the two of them slip out of the bushes. For a moment they stand there looking dumb as drywall, topless like a couple of Viking hippies. My wife-but-not-really-my-wife is wearing red cowboy boots. What the fuck has this Viking done to her? She moves her hands to cover her breasts which are larger than I remember, and opens her mouth to scream, from joy no doubt that I have come to rescue her, to take her away from this savage who ruined our lives.

I drum up my best John Wayne voice. "Get some clothes on. This is a raid."

I step towards her and hold out my hand.

"Oh my God," she mumbles. Even her voice is different.

Then the Viking, with a smear of sunscreen on his nose and a tie-dye shirt wrapped around his waist, steps between us. One look and I know he's the kind of asshole with a real nice sprinkler system to keep his lawn green while everything else goes to dust. He tosses his glasses into the sand and tackles me.

After a few punches I can tell something is wrong. He looks strange. Scrawny. He has no tattoos. Fuck. No blond hair. No pelt of skins. No beard. Not a Viking. Fuck. Not the man I am looking for.

"Pervert," he grunts as we wrestle.

"What have you done?" my fake wife says over and over. She's holding baby girl who is now crying.

I already know what happens next before it happens. It's the same movie all over again. I only wish baby girl didn't have to see me like this. I want to be hit again. Please. I live for it. This is all I have. You sonfabitch. Hit me. Knock me senseless. Please.

Thankfully, the fake Viking hits me. The world spins upside-down and I am a thread hanging from it. Then I feel my baseball bat crack down on my legs. It crushes my chest. It feels like popcorn kernels exploding in my guts. Then here comes Winston slithering to the rescue.

"Kill it!" my fake wife screams.

The baseball bat goes up and down.

I lay on the sandbar breathing heavy, spitting up blood. The fake Viking looks on the verge of tears. His hands tremble. He doesn't know it, but I saved him.

"Pervert!" the wannabe Viking yells.

———————

When I open my eyes, I'm on the mud bank where the fake Viking left me. The desert feels hot on my face. Winston's mutilated body is here too. Kneeling, I try to put him back together.

"Don't worry, Winston," I whisper, his orange insides spilling between my fingers. "We'll find a wizard to put you together. We'll follow the cards and find some real magic."

I open his mouth and give him two quick breaths.

My hands smell like baby girl piss. It was her. It was. It had to be.

Then sirens, lights, and voices on the road. Fuck the police, Big Frida always says.

Downstream. That's where the cards say the fools go. I float. I can feel the Virgin getting shallow. Like she's running away. Like she's drying up into a sick yellow paste. Like she can't heal thieves like me. I put my lips to her and tell her I'm sorry. I tell her I'm the marshmallow man. I tell her tomorrow I'll bring her more water. I can save her. I sing her Elmore James. I sing *when things go wrong, go wrong with you, it hurts me too*. Farther downstream a strange glow lights up the Virgin. We move through the vanishing waters, slipping between shadows and other ghosts.

The Jump Humping
Handbook for Dummies

1. The problem is physics.

2. As my performance reviews indicate, I exceed proficiency in hygiene, punctuality, theoretical modeling, and inconspicuous ambiance. My problem is physics: Newton, the apple, light bending through prisms into rainbows and whatnot. And vibration. Amplitude, frequency, acceleration. I should have known better. My mother enrolled me in a retro hip-hop dance class when I was a girl believing I was destined for the *Star Search* reboot with animatronic Ed McMahon, but the dance instructor said fat white girls don't have the rhythm to do the Roger Rabbit. It's a fact.

3. *You are a daughter of Eve,* the intercom voice tells me during morning prayers, *the first oscillator.*

4. But am I? Most days I feel like Schrödinger's tuning fork.

5. I could blame the heartstopper. Or as I described it in my recent self-eval, the one that got me refracted

back down to the 31st floor, the Anomalous Metaphysical Experience.

6. Listen. I'm not one of these people who wants to see the metaphysical. I like to keep the physics in my life of the less than meta sort. True, I used to visit Las Vegas twice a year—for the buffets, not the nightlife, except maybe the Wayne Newton hologram which happens to be the closest thing we have to heaven— but otherwise I am not a phantasmagoric kind of girl who enjoys malfeasance. I am twenty-nine, Sagittarius, unvaccinated, and still a virgin. I prefer the anomalies in my life to be good feasance.

7. I live in the Institute. Downtown next to the temple. It's shaped like a beehive. Each floor a tapering spiral stacked on the previous with hundreds of honey-combed cells full of apprentices like me studying to be jump humpers.

8. Proof No. 9: *I will remember there is soaking and there is jump humping and see that all things be done in wisdom and order.*

9. It was my boyfriend who taught me about soaking. It's the most Mormon thing imaginable. A man and a woman in flagrante delicto. Only the key inserted into the lock without turning. The key perfectly still, soaking.

10. A loophole in God's fornication policy.

11.   My boyfriend invented it. I never learned his name.
       Only that he was tired of being like every other par-
       ticle in the universe, passing through town on his way
       to places unknown. The earth is spinning a thousand
       miles per hour and even now, he said pointing to the
       stars, endless heavens are folding up like a scroll and
       worlds without end are fading into a cosmic smear.

12.   Let's be still, he said.

13.   We got nude as scallops in the motel. While we soaked,
       he told me things. Inside the atom is the electron,
       the proton, the neutron, my boyfriend said. Inside
       those are quarks and muons. Inside those are neutri-
       nos. The ghost particles. Inside ghosts are tiny strings
       that vibrate endlessly.

14.   It's ghosts all the way down, he said.

15.   It was our second date. He proposed an hour later. It
       was beautiful.

16.   Proof No. 3: *I will begin all jump humping with a prayer.*

17.   There are soakers in my bed. Specialty simulation
       mannequins so we can perfect our jump humping
       techniques. Less dolls than animatronic puppets. Very
       lifelike and full of the appropriate fluids to simulate
       real bodies.

18.   Every room in the Institute is equipped with two
       mannequins. I don't tell them they're mannequins, of
       course. I call them Adam and Eve.

19. Adam will make various grunts and sighs and wheez-
     ings when properly stimulated. Eve has flexible limbs,
     no voice box. Maybe she was manufactured this way,
     or it's an assembly defect, or perhaps an accident like
     when I was on the 14th floor and jump humped too
     zealously. The Adam short-circuited, catching the Eve
     on fire.

20. I watched them burn.

21. That was my first demotion. REFRACTION, the per-
     formance evaluation said in bright red letters.

22. This place used to be Utah. Now we've rebranded.
     Deseret Nation, the flag says. Where soaking is the
     only permissible marriage sacrament and the science
     of jump humping will save us.

23. Proof No. 11: *I am only an oscillator, not the*
     primum movens.

24. I perform anywhere between ten to five hundred jump
     humping simulations per day. Every morning I wake
     up and find Adam and Eve soaking in one of the four-
     teen Church-approved positions. Missionary, flatiron,
     reverse cowgirl, Butter Churner, Sphinx, Snow Angel,
     Crooked Spoon, etc. My job is to crawl beneath the
     bed and oscillate it in such a way to bring them to
     climax without the two of them ever moving volun-
     tarily. They soak, I jump hump. This is the system.

25. I have sixty seconds between sessions. Rest. Recuperate. Repeat. I keep my eye on the clock.

26. We are human vibrators. Batteries not included.

27. Adam is not what I expected. Neanderthal forehead, bearded, slim, a wonky eyelid that flutters when I jump hump as if he's winking, and generously endowed albeit hooked, like a donkey. It detaches. The handbook says this is abnormal, but Adam doesn't seem to mind.

28. Sometimes I use it to scratch my back. You know that spot? The one right under the shoulder blade that always hurts but is impossible to reach?

29. Eve's eyes are glued shut.

30. Proof No. 71: *I will abstain from worldly lusts, transforming my garden into a beehive for the Lord.*

31. When Adam first came apart, I thought I'd broken him. Scrolled up inside his detachable were instructions for his appropriate care and use: *Lonely white male more lovable than E.T. looking for mentally-stable, disease-free quiet woman who speaks in tongues to share long walks on the beach. Must be equal parts undiluted love and charm with a generous heaping of honesty. Must be modest in dress and spirit and averse to heavy petting or other unwholesome recreations. Must love flea markets and lunar libations. Must love fruit.*

32.   There are no instructions for Eve.

33.   Which means she doesn't know anything about being a woman. How you must spend your day playing games and winning tickets like at the arcade, but when you get to the trade-in counter all the prizes are cheap plastic trinkets that fall apart after two seconds.

34.   Sometimes after a simulation I'll hold up Eve's face to my own in the mirror. Our hair is cut almost the same and were it not for the cigarette burn scars on my thighs like old arabesque wallpaper and her garden which is much better pruned than mine, I might forget which of us is real and which of us is synthetic. Luckily, her foot is stamped: MADE IN INDONESIA.

35.   God is kind and gentle and loving, I tell Eve, but he's just a small thing in the chaos of the universe. Look around. This is the best he could do.

36.   The Mormons say one day we too can be gods with a world of our own. But I think we're already gods. Dressed up in these human skin costumes trying to remember what it's like to feel.

37.   And then my sixty seconds are over, and it's back to the problem of physics.

38.   Proof No. 17: *I will remain blindfolded during all sim-ulations, for when we are blind then we can see.*

39.   I teach Eve lots of words: witch, Madonna, crone, maiden, mystic, midwife, harlot, huntress, spinster, priestess. Most girls only get one of these words, I tell her, unless you learn how to babayaga them. A word after a word after a word makes a soul.

40.   I don't have many words for the Anomalous Metaphysical Experience.

41.   We were on a shift break when my boyfriend said, Let me cook you a Big H triple-chili-cheeseburger with the special sauce, and then I knew he was one of them. The Three Nephites. That old Mormon legend of the spiritual gurus who wander the earth like those Scottish highlanders friends with Sean Connery.

42.   But how can you be sure an indigenous Israeli-Mormon convert from the Yucatan alive these last two thousand years and fixing flat tires for stranded motorists up and down I-15 to prepare for Christ's second coming is working as a short order cook at the Big H? And how do you know he will teach you the true order of intercourse?

43.   Six-foot-five, mocha skin, hair like Bon Jovi, and a Peter Pan tattoo on his forearm. I'd recognize the Lord's disciples anywhere.

44.   Besides, only ancient Mormon prophets have beards like that.

45.   They call it a heartstopper, I said, licking the chili off my fingers, that ever happen to you? It won't be your

heart that stops, he said. I wanted to ask what that meant, but then he winked and said, You ever hear of soaking?

46. Proof No. 4: *I will jump hump for Jesus, not pleasure. In His name will I oscillate the population back from the brink of extinction.*

47. When I informed my bishop about the Anomalous Metaphysical Experience, he had me write a detailed complaint—confession, he called it—and assured me it would make its way up the Church chain of command. The next thing I knew I was at the Institute surrounded by physics with an itch I couldn't scratch.

48. Proof No. 5: *I will not deviate from my instruction, for obedience is the first law of heaven.*

49. *The body is a temple*, the intercom voice reminds us every evening. But really it is an attic crawlspace full of somebody else's ghosts. The future is in squatting.

50. Proof No. 31: *I will be paid in blessings, the exchange rate to be determined post–Rapture.*

51. It could be I'm delusional. I have trouble sleeping. I used to count sheep but now I rehearse my proofs. There are ninety-five in the handbook, one revealed on every floor of the Institute.

52. I am making my own handbook. Recorded one whisper at a time into Eve's circuits in sixty second intervals.

53. I used to believe that one day I'd graduate and be
     rented out from one family to another, jump humping
     our Deseret Nation back from population collapse.
     But now I know I'll never leave the Institute. But Eve
     might. Back to the garden for reprogramming.

54. I wish I could see the look on their faces when they
     dissect her motherboard and find the malware that
     is me.

55. Don't forget to bite that apple, I whisper in her ani-
     matronic ear. Sink your teeth into it first so your
     daughters will know the new physics.

56. Other times I'll look out my window and try to count
     all the soakers in this desert. Thousands of them right
     now, everyone connected by stillness. So still they're
     not even sure they're alive.

57. Proof No. 10: *I will neither shake nor tremble nor jiggle
     nor wobble nor gyrate nor quiver the bed. I will move it
     with the faith of a mustard seed.*

58. Once when I couldn't sleep I put the Adam in the
     closet and spooned with Eve. I told her about the time
     I won the tickets at the arcade playing the Whack-a-
     Worm. The one with the mechanical worm that pops
     out of the hole and if you smack it with the mallet
     it glows.

59. They looked like the tongue worms the goats used to
     get on the farm when I was a girl. We'd find the goats

out in the fields all hollowed out inside. The worms had magic tongues, my daddy used to say, given to them by God. They were always swallowing, burrowing labyrinthine tunnels through liver and lungs and brains until there was nothing left.

60. The day I won all the tickets the game malfunctioned. The worms popped up but never went back down into the hole. I tried to break them, but the more I clubbed the brighter they glowed.

The Algorithms of Happiness

The woman they call the Leech moves through the rooms unnoticed, removing dirty vials from machines and placing them gently in her biohazard cart. She wants nothing more than to take these into the decontamination room and sterilize them, but she knows her protocols. She knows there must be order in all things.

She removes the plastic tubes and hoses. She removes the aluminum sheets and fifty other metallic parts whose names she learned but has since forgotten. She disassembles the gears and arranges them carefully on the floor for inspection. Then, slowly, she begins to clean.

Scrub, flush, wipe, scour, rinse, mop, dust, disinfect. There are so many words for cleaning but only a single word for dreaming. This bothers the Leech. There should be more words. Why isn't there a job to name the unnamable things? She knows this is a dangerous question, because to name is to feel and she has no time to dwell on such misfortunes. She stands. The room is white, sterile. She arranges disinfectants in her cart. She catches a reflection of herself in the window but moves quickly out the door. There are a dozen other machines to clean tonight and so many fluids to discard.

____

The Leech is not aware who discovered the process. Maybe it was invented, not discovered. The Leech is not sure of the difference. It happened long before she was born, back when they still called this place Utah. At first the scientists believed they had discovered the soul. Only later did they realize the fluids extracted from the brain using the machine were emotions. A fifth state of matter, the scientists declared. So, after years of blackening skies—after the pesticides and the plastics and the chemtrails and the melted ice caps— they went public with the discovery and announced the first desiporium. An emporium of desires, of feelings, the mayor announced, where people could choose whatever emotions they wanted. HAPPINESS IN THREE DROPS!

Who could resist?

Who would imagine such a process? the Leech wonders as she cleans. It doesn't matter. What matters, the Leech tells herself, is the process is remarkable, just as she is unremarkable.

In the next room she disassembles another machine, sterilizes it. She soaks up spilled emotions with the mop. It's a shame, the Leech thinks, a woman is not a machine that can be taken apart and put back together again.

____

The Leech did not choose her nickname. A janitor, technically, but she prefers Leech. She does not protest the indignity of names. Hers is a noble profession. Little things are consequential too, she remembers hearing in training. She wears a dark gray jumpsuit. Her hair is always pinned up in a bun. Whenever she walks through the hallway others step out of her way, pressing their backs to the wall, afraid to touch her.

———————

The Leech pushes the cart slowly past the windows on her way to the next donation room. At this hour, the city is quiet. A place of wind and dust where all the streets are curveless and light is infrequent. It is that hour of night not quite twilight and not quite dawn, the time when animals dream. Strangely, it pleases her that while others dream she must clean.

———————

She did not ever imagine becoming a Leech. As a girl, the only thing she enjoyed was diving to the bottom of the lake, her father pulling her up until one day he was no longer there. Even now she will run a hot bath after a shift and slip underwater, counting how long she can hold her breath.

———————

The Chief Designer who interviewed her for the position at the facility, the desiporium they call it, asked only a single question: What is your favorite emotion? She could tell this was a man who had never sunk to the bottom of a lake and screamed. If we're being honest, the Leech said, I feel very little.

The donors are pleasant but messy. Kneeling, the Leech scrubs the floors of footprints, dirt, flakes of skin, crusts, jellies, and whatever liquefied emotions have been left behind by the process. The Leech likes the look of cleanliness, just as she likes the look of sickness. Each one reaching for the other but never touching, like rings on a tree stump. Under a gurney she discovers two pale amber drops, like juice from an apricot. Sometimes when cleaning she pauses, wondering to whom these drops belonged, trying to picture the face of the donor. This too is dangerous. To imagine is to feel.

She wipes up the drops with a sponge, careful not to let it touch her skin. Once she carelessly and accidentally wiped the sweat from her forehead with the back of her hand, not knowing there was a drop of turquoise. She spent the rest of the night feeling shy, so painfully shy she locked herself in the closet. Her supervisor sent her home and suspended her for a week without pay. Luckily, she and her mother had saved a few cans of food under the floorboard in case of emergency.

On the counter is a drop of guilt. Every emotion has its own color. Pomegranates, azures, golds, and greens. Indexed and coded. She had to memorize a color chart in training. Surprise is purple. Disgust is yellow. Shame comes in various hues of orange depending on the potency. Once extracted from donors, emotions in the liquid state are seldom pure, always an intense swirl, uneasily separated by another machine upstairs which the Leech is not allowed to see or clean. Each emotion is given to a technician for distillation. The Leech doesn't know how to distill emotions. She only knows how to sterilize and dispose of them. But she is learning.

From her pocket, the Leech unfolds a string of paper dolls like an accordion. Each is a slightly different color, like a sad rainbow. Sometimes she likes to pretend this is her family. Sometimes lying in bed she will stare at these dolls for hours. She knows she could dissolve the paper dolls in water and take a cocktail of emotion, slipping off into an endless dream. But the Leech has watched television programs about animals surviving in the wild, about mothers who eat their young. *Because of mercy*, the voice on the program says. And so, the Leech only looks at the paper dolls, saving them for something merciful.

After looking over her shoulder, the Leech dabs the doll into the drop. The paper turns pale burgundy. Folding the dolls and wrapping them in plastic, she returns them to her pocket.

———

The Leech polishes the machine until it shines. Before becoming the Leech, she never considered the body is a house of many fluids. It always seemed to her like a piece of paper waiting to be folded then torn, but never a place of dwelling, of permanence.

———

It was a classmate at the school for unclean girls—the school where a girl goes to learn how to be a Leech—who taught the Leech how to look. The Leech doesn't remember her name. Never look at anything straight on, the girl said. That's suicide. Always glimpse. That's the only way to know if what you're seeing is real. If you're a boy you can look without blinking. But you and me, well, we're not so lucky.

The Leech cleans the windows, her hand moving in circles, leaving behind no streaks. Below are rows of black rooftops like teeth crowded inside a mouth. Without needing to squint she can see dozens of other desiporiums scattered over the city, their identical chimneys leaking yellow vapor. In every one a Leech just like her cleaning up the mess of the day's spilled emotions.

She's lost track of how many years she's been leeching. Since her mother got sick. It used to be so exhilarating, the leeching. The aromas, the noise, the mess. So many people, such emotion, such wonder. The world was new again. She liked cleaning up leftover drops of surprise. It left joyful streaks on the floor. She liked boredom. It stained. She was indifferent to hope, a frequent donation. Now she is tired of all this feeling. Isn't it better to think than to feel? During her breaks she sips coffee and thinks enormous nothings of thought.

The Leech pauses the cleaning cart outside one of the donation rooms. She is not supposed to watch the process, but she cannot help but watch. The technicians wear heavy leather aprons and safety goggles. A sign on every wall says, THAT

THEY MIGHT HAVE JOY. Even with the safety equipment the process turns the technicians' hair slightly luminescent, as if they've been dipped in moonlight. Donors sit inside the machine, blindfolded, legs secured in stirrups, suction cups applied all over their head. Soft music plays. The technician counts backwards signaling the donor to bring into focus whatever memory is the vessel for donation. If they are donating rage they must conjure up a memory full of rage. Sadness requires sad thoughts. And so on. The fresher the memory the more potent the extracted emotion and the more money the donor will be paid. When it's over, the emotion is distilled into a vial, but the memory is lost.

The technician uses the foot pedal to adjust the extraction pressure in the suction cups. The machine gurgles. There is steam and hissing. Slowly, the fluid drips out into the vials. It looks rather painless.

After, when she comes into the room for cleanup, the Leech feels invisible. Invisible is not the same as ghosted, she knows. Microbes. A jellyfish heart. Ex-boyfriends. Such ghosts do not excite her. She prefers invisible things. Peeling a mandarin in one peel. Riding down an elevator. God. The Leech would like to believe in God. She pictures him as a switchboard operator, cigarette dangling between his lips as if he's one of those detectives in a black and white film. He pushes buttons. The lights light up telling him which plugs need connections to new ports. She wonders which one of those ports is her mother. Her mother whose laugh used to disturb the stars, who knew how to cook happiness into a spoonful of pie, her mother who requires three drops under the tongue to keep her mind from yesterday or tomorrow as she sits in front of the television all day wrapped in a blanket, a little drool at the corner of her mouth. Her mother loves that television, always asking it how it slept first thing in the morning, polishing the screen, dusting the cables. How many times has the Leech come home from her shift to find the picture fuzzy and her mother singing it lullabies?

In her head, the Leech sees God's fingers fumble as he hurries to connect the switchboard plugs. There's static. Suddenly, it all goes dark. What does God do, the Leech wonders, now that the algorithms of happiness have spun out of his control?

———————

Three drops of blue on the floor. The Leech saves these with her paper dolls. She has never donated her emotions. She imagines if she did it would be a sea of blue. There are a million shades of melancholy, but twice as many shades of pain, each of them named and numbered, because people are not satisfied with their own pain. They want to exchange it for the pain of others, perhaps believing it is more manageable, or perhaps because there is such pleasure in someone else's misery.

———————

Her father was a dentist. As a girl, she used to clean the tools in his office. Scalers, bristles, forceps, keys. He taught her how to use them. He showed her anatomy books with pictures of teeth and palatopharyngeal arches and tongues. He taught her pain. Did you know there are two billion nerve endings in the human mouth? Pain is an elevator. This, he said, tracing the metallic hook along her gums, is one. This, he said, piercing the tip into the uvula, is five. And this, he said, clenching a molar with pliers and beginning to pull, is nine.

———————

There is so much pain, she came to understand. And there is not enough pain.

———————

The Leech knows she should leave. She clocked out an hour ago. Her mother is waiting, no doubt dizzied from watching fourteen hours of televised dog racing, waiting for her to put the three drops under her tongue. But the Leech loves peeking into the lobby. There are two entries to every desiporium. One facing the street for customers. One in the alley for donors. In the lobby is where the vials of emotions are shelved floor to ceiling. The glass bottles catch the light and spread against the walls in an eerie phosphorescence, like being inside a kaleidoscope.

Wouldn't it be nice to go through the door facing the street? To walk up to the counter and request whatever vial you wanted? Six drops now, four drops later. Wouldn't it be nice to have the luxury of perfectly measured feeling? The scientists warn against too much emotion, saying the brain can't process it, saying it can be fatal. But still. It would be nice to feel, the Leech thinks. And it would be nice to be free from the burden of feeling.

Leave, she tells herself. But she loves the look of strange light. She loves the quiet hum of the machines. She loves the feel of clean things under her feet. She stays for pleasure, for the pleasure of *it*.

———————

And then she sees him. A man, a boy really, with a face full of wrinkles pacing outside the revolving door. He wears a blue threadbare suit. No tie. Frayed collar. Not even twenty, the Leech thinks, his skin is already sallowed. It's rare for donors to visit at this hour. There are no appointments. Only walk-ins. The Leech knows the ones who come at this hour are desperate, if they know they are here at all.

The Leech used to pity the donors. Now she guards her emotions, caging them in tiny knots within her chest. The world is sick. Feeling is harder than it used to be. She knows if she feels she will be tempted to donate. And once you begin donating you never stop.

The man shuffles into the lobby. It is his third time tonight. The law says you can only donate twice a week, but there are loopholes. Donors at this hour all look the same, like scarecrows in January. Once hooked into the machines they become floppers, floaters, spitters, singers, shakers, moaners, biters, screamers, tremblers, and laughers. It's not easy to extract someone's feelings. They leave a mess on the floor. But without a mess there is no Leech and if there is no leeching then she is not and if she is not then how can she think these incredible nothings of thought?

Whenever the Leech sees a donor, it ghosts her heart.

———————

The Leech hurries across the lobby floor and takes the man by the arm. She has no idea why she acts this way.

There's room for one more, the Leech says quietly.

Behind the curtain she helps the man into the machine, strapping him into the stirrups and tightening the suctions around his head. She blindfolds him.

Hold still, the Leech says. Think about your memory.

When will it begin? the dazed man whispers.

Soon, the Leech says. Try to relax.

The machine begins to hum. The man trembles. The Leech wonders what is going on inside his mind. The Leech wants to believe he is thinking about his mother. Maybe his mother never hugged him too, just shook his hand at bedtime. Maybe he too found embraces in other things: climbing trees, or lying on train tracks, or crawling inside the abandoned boiler on a summer day and feeling the sweat pool on his skin. The man's mouth is open but there are no words coming out. It's shocking, the Leech thinks, how you can erase someone and not even know it.

His skin is brittle from too much donation, like his body is being sucked dry. She thinks about her mother at home. The church elders tried to have her institutionalized after she claimed she saw one of the lizard-folk with a six-foot tail showering in the Salt Lake temple. That's when the Leech got a job at the desiporium to pay for the extra medication. Sometimes she'll come home and find her mother has scratched her thighs bloody trying to make sure she's not made of scales.

Gently, she'll coax open her mother's mouth. One, two, three drops under the tongue.

A soft, not quite pink liquid trickles into the vial. The Leech knows all the colors of the emotion spectrum but has never seen a color like this before. It hurts to look at it. She does not blink.

The Leech wonders what it would be like to put two, maybe eleven drops of this new emotion under her mother's tongue? Nobody would ever know. What emotion could it be? The sudden feeling of your own smallness? The sadness of knowing you were born in the wrong place and the wrong time? The frustration of realizing in your brief life you will live a fraction of human experience? It could be anything. The fear and joy of walking on the rings of Saturn. The longing not for the past or future but an alternative present, the longing for elsewhere. The heartache for a sideways world whose algorithms are yours but not yours.

Outside the roads are dusty and empty. The Leech wonders what animal is dreaming her. It would be nice if it was something small, she thinks, like a rabbit or a shrew, something quiet and forgettable, something ghosted but not yet invisible.

Is it over? the man mumbles. Soft pink tears trickle down his cheeks. The Leech soaks these up with the paper dolls.

Not yet, the Leech says. Focus. Just a little bit more.

She clasps the man's hand in her own.

She does not blink.

Breathe, the Leech says as she presses the foot pedal, gentle at first and then almost grinding it into the floor. The machine hums. The suction cups hiss. It will be such a mess, the Leech smiles. The man's mouth opens. Small gasps leave his lips. One. Two. Three. And together they bring the drops into this world of clean sick things.

Forecasts

Expect mild temperatures between 4 September and 18 September, followed by a period of unusual warmth. Expect light rains, especially before the gibbous moon. First frosts will be after the equinox. Venus will be the ruling planet. The Virgin watches over all. Avoid citrus. Tread carefully with common-law wives. Lucky numbers: 9, 14, 19, 27. Expect Olaf Yorgensen to win top prize at the Fourth Annual Jigglefest Jell-O extravaganza.

Expect the factory to close unexpectedly. Workers will tear up pink slips. About a mile down the road, expect Mrs. Talbot to fetch the wash on the clothesline at approximately 4:58 P.M., just as her neighbor, Kitty Nielsen, is handcuffing herself to machinery inside the factory. Mrs. Talbot will wrangle towels away from the children who have spent the afternoon pretending the towels are rafts and spacecrafts and superhero capes. She will pause as she finds the other garments still hanging are slightly damp, soiled with the unmistakable scent of urine.

Expect minor atmospheric disturbances. Solar flares will be likely. Representatives from the Observatory will meet with concerned residents to address their concerns. Precautions will be necessary, but no health risks are anticipated.

Expect Wilbur Baum, sketch artist for the police, to receive a suspicious letter in the mail. The letter will contain scraps of damp paper with scribbled chemical equations. They will smell of urine. Wilbur Baum will stand several minutes on the sidewalk, barefoot, hands sticky as he glances at the menacing equations, bewildered and wondering what kind of game is being played.

Expect sunrise at 6:37 A.M. and sunset at 7:02 P.M.

Expect Ms. Bennion to return to the parking lot after her shift at the Observatory and find her car door ajar. Nothing will be stolen. Both the driver's seat and the passenger seat will be damp. Probably from the sprinklers, Ms. Bennion will guess. Three minutes later she will notice the odor. Stale but rancid. Some bastard, she will tell authorities, pissed in her car. She will go to the laundromat. Waiting for the police to arrive she will strip down to her underwear and stand, slightly ashamed, listening to the spin cycle.

Expect Wilbur Baum to visit the library. He will sit in a chair facing the window with a yearbook in his lap. He will think about the fourth grade and Kammy Stucki. He will remember the playground, the tetherball, how she wore a blue blouse with a plaid skirt. Two ropes of braided hair half-concealing a teasing smile. Without warning she kissed him. It was soft and sloppy. Wilbur Baum stood there, unable to move when suddenly she bit his lips. Hard. He will remember the bleeding. Even now he will taste blood unexpectedly. He will go to the bathroom and spit in the sink. He will remember screaming. He will remember how Kammy Stucki, like a wild animal, clenched down. They laughed at him for wetting himself. Wetting Wilbur. That was his name through high school. No girl would kiss him until college. Wilbur Baum will skim through the yearbook pages. The high school reunion will be next month. Grudges can last a lifetime, Wilbur Baum's wife will tell him. Love too, he will say.

Expect a woman wearing pastel culottes and a floppy straw hat to post a sign on the rec center office window indicating the town pool will be closed until further notice. Orange biohazard stickers will be placed over the doors. It will be called a toxic liquid event in the *Tribune*. The lifeguard noticed a murky yellow hue in the pool and evacuated the senior citizen Water Warrior aerobics class. One woman fainted. Another, in the panic, slipped and cracked a tooth. Witnesses will come forward saying a trespassing occurred the night previous. One will say the trespasser was a female child, nine to eleven years. Another will say an adult male with dark skin, possibly with a mustache.

Expect a preliminary report on the 6 P.M. news: MYSTERY URINATOR IN TOWN?

Expect at least three children in Ms. Wambaugh's fifth-grade classroom to give their weekly history reports on urine. Jessie Pilkington will report General Custer would have triumphed at Little Bighorn had his men made gunpowder from urine like Custer had been told in a dream. Jessie Pilkington will spray the front row of the class with his squirt gun. The children will scream. Ms. Wambaugh will award him a C+ for *creative but questionable history*.

Expect crowds to march around the factory chanting as they wave banners and fist the air. Expect someone will throw a brick.

Expect the public health department to issue an announcement regarding sanitary precautions when encountering urine. *All public urine outside of designated receptacles is in violation of town ordinances.* Following the commercial break, the weatherman will say Napoleon was a notorious bedwetter. The morning of Waterloo he awoke to find the bed dry, believing it a favorable omen. The other news anchors will nod their heads in unison with quizzical but earnest stares.

Expect Wilbur Baum will fix the ham radio in the basement. He will sit there all evening listening to static and eavesdropping on police dispatches. He will sketch faces, trying to imagine the kind of face that goes with each voice. He will remember sketching faces of shoplifters when he was nine and getting paid a dollar for each one. He will remember sketching Ginny Merrill after she was strangled behind the bowling alley. He will remember sketching Patty Udall who was fished out the lake with brine shrimp for eyes. He will remember his wife's face on the Ferris wheel and how he undrew her with his eyes. He will remember Orson Zabriskie, whose wife clubbed him with a skillet then cooked eggs while waiting for the police. He will remember when he was a Mormon missionary and sketched a man in a retirement home who may or may not have been wearing a Yeti costume, but as he sketched the Yeti sprawled out on the bed with the saddest and most beautiful look on his face, nobody could pull the costume off. He will wonder why some things of the mind are a tissue of dreams and others an anvil. Now almost sixty, Wilbur Baum will be ready for a different kind of crime. He will take long lunch breaks and eye people using public restrooms, wondering if they too hesitate before the toilet, straining to force out a few drops.

OCTOBER

Expect a sudden shift in temperatures beginning 9 October. Expect a large turnout for this year's reenactment of the Mountain Meadows Massacre. Expect average harvests of corn, soy, and sorghum. Yields of apples will be abundant. Pluto will be the ruling planet. The Scales will not balance. Choose the high road or the low road, but a choice will be made, same as a fisherman reeling in his net. Avoid moths, excessive laughter, and the light of a waxing moon. Neither seek nor fear the jackalope. Lucky numbers: 4, 11, 42, 96.

Expect only seven boys from the Little League team will come to practice. One of the boys, Hyrum Pratt, will collapse on the diamond and flop in the dirt like a fish, his skin pale as an oyster after it's been cracked and all the brine spills out. Foam will bubble on his lips. The ambulance will haul him away. The park will be empty. One boy will be left behind. He will stare at the shape of his friend left in the dirt. He will think it looks yellowed. By the time his mother arrives an hour late he will have wet himself twice.

Expect Wilbur Baum to file a complaint with the post office. With some difficulty, he will try to remember the postman's face who delivered the suspicious letter but will only conjure vague details. Chapped lips, gaunt, pigeon-chested with wavy hair, thin mustache. The postmaster, itching the top of his bald head, will inform Wilbur Baum nobody fitting that description delivers mail. How is it our sketch artist can't remember a face? the postmaster will laugh. Maybe we should tell the feds, Wilbur Baum will say quietly, just in case. The postmaster laughs. This is Utah. What could possibly happen? he will laugh, then tell Wilbur Baum he's lucky it's just wet paper because not everyone is so fortunate. Sometimes other things are delivered. Terrorists? Wilbur Baum will whisper. The postmaster will lean close. Dog shit, he will say.

Expect a library patron to check out an old medical textbook, *Crisfeld's Encyclopedia of Peculiar Medical Disorders and How to Cure Them*. On page 387, the librarian, a certain Ms. Lucy Meacham, will discover damp, sticky pages with multiple stains. Fourteen other volumes will be removed from circulation having been similarly violated. News vans will roll up. It's spreading, the librarians will say.

Expect Abagail Woolley to sit on a bus stop bench. The skies will be sunny. She will stand suddenly, eyeing a puddle on the bench. It just rained, a man will say. Abagail Woolley will hyperventilate, convinced she is infected.

Expect vigils at the park. One for the Pratt boy who collapsed playing baseball. One for the authorities to apprehend the mysterious urinator.

Expect a press conference with the sheriff. Let's get one thing straight, he will say trying to quell the hysteria, nobody is infected. There is no infection. It's only urine. It's just stains.

Expect sunrise at 7:14 A.M. and sunset at 6:28 P.M.

Expect a fluctuation in tides to have significant impact on health. Teeth will ache. Rashes will get worse before they get better. Wilbur Baum will sit on a pew in the back of the chapel, alone, like he always does. He will resist the urge to take out his sketchpad and draw the face of God. Instead, he will stare at his fellow worshippers. Some dozing off, some listening to the silence, some waiting like birds with broken wings perched on the edge of a cliff. He will wonder if any of them is the face of God. He will stare at the pulpit, empty, waiting for someone to bear testimony. He will want to be that person. He will want to be touched by the holy spirit and say beautiful things, like, *fear not*, like, *God's hand designs all things, even serial urinators.*

Expect Jody Harmon and Wendell Brandt, both high school seniors, to sneak out of their houses and rendezvous near the chapel. They will ignore the biohazard sticker and slip under the police tape surrounding the bus stop shelter. They will smile. They will kiss.

Expect the sheriff to stand in the room as Wilbur Baum finishes the facial sketch. Can't you make his face more perverted? the sheriff will ask.

Expect Norman Bickerstaff to collect signatures to place a moratorium on urinating within the town limits. They're infecting us! he will cry, waving the clipboard inside the library. When asked how he intends to enforce such a policy, Norman Bickerstaff will tilt his chin and narrow his eyes. There are ways, he will say with a quiet menace.

Expect the fruit festival to be phenomenal. Expect there to be peaches and cherries and huckleberries and plums. Expect a crowd to approach Seymour Brunson's booth. Instead of fruit he will display glass vials of what looks like lemon juice. What is it? someone will ask. Urine, Seymour Brunson will say. Who needs urine? someone else will ask, laughing. An aphrodisiac. Sure, buddy. *The* urine, Seymour Brunson will say. A hush will fall over the crowd. Does it work? It will cost you, Seymour Brunson will say. You're selling it? Step aside, Seymour Brunson will say, this is a business. People will come forward with cash in their trembling hands.

Expect the factory workers to set up a tent city in the parking lot. At night they will burn fires in barrels and share hot apple cider. In the mornings they huddle in prayer circles, but the news cameras don't record this.

Expect the fire marshal's wife to awake at 2:14 A.M. and prepare herself a cup of chamomile tea. Following tea, she will use the toilet and discover the bowl brimming with urine. The fire marshal's wife, Irene Pulsipher, will maintain it is not her urine, nor that of her husband whose urine she is much acquainted with after thirty-four years of marriage. The sight of the amber liquid will give her a headache, but she will not be able to look away. There will be no freckled spray on the porcelain, no droplets left behind on the tile. Either he cleaned up his mess or is a remarkable urinator, she will tell authorities. She will entertain the idea the urinator is a woman, as only a woman could be so precise. Her husband, the fire marshal, will advise her not to get carried away with fantasies.

Expect the sheriff will hold a press conference with an update on the serial urinator. He will release Wilbur Baum's sketch of a slim mustachioed man but will caution: It could be anyone. Someone you know, maybe even someone you love. A reporter will question the sheriff: could it be you? The sheriff will chuckle.

Expect Wilbur Baum to find it difficult to believe Irene Pulsipher's testimony. Whereas the previous incidents will be marked with playful charm, this will feel different. It will frighten him, such misanthropic genius. Being a guest in a neighbor's bathroom is a solemn responsibility. Wilbur Baum knows there are rigorous standards of etiquette. That trust will have been violated. He will fear nothing is safe going forward. Using the toilet will feel scandalous. It has always been embarrassing, but now he will perform his bodily functions with reverent unease. For as much as he will wish to admit he is nothing like the urinator, every visit to the toilet will serve as a reminder of their shared nature. Wilbur Baum will forever acknowledge he owes the urinator a strange debt of gratitude which can never be fully repaid. Did you say something? Lavinia Baum will say at the dinner table. No, Wilbur Baum will say, I said nothing.

Expect a mustachioed man will be tackled at the park. The two men will struggle in the grass. *Citizen's arrest*! Frank Yorgensen will shout. Pinned down by three other men, the mustachioed man will scream for help, will insist he is not a pervert, he is not sick, he is not sick.

Expect birthday parties to be postponed. Expect neighbors to eye each other suspiciously in the grocery aisle. Expect many to stop attending church services, but Wilbur Baum will persist. His ancestors were Mormon pioneers who crossed the plains with the prophet Brigham Young and fought off the Paiutes and survived cholera and agonized over unanswered prayers. When a small boy drinks water from a sacrament cup and whispers *this tastes like piss* and people frantically begin to shuffle out the doors, Wilbur Baum will drink a second cup of sacrament water.

Expect a college student walking up the library steps to be approached by a well-groomed man who will give her a brief but intense hug. The attack will last a few seconds. The suspect will release her, saying he had mistaken her for someone else, then flee the scene. During routine medical examination, paramedics will notice damp stains on the college student's clothing. She will claim she was not frightened and did not wet herself, but it was possible the hugger had urinated on her. Authorities will quickly rule out this incident as the work of the serial urinator. A urinator and a hugger, the sheriff will say, are two very different things.

Expect the local news station to begin a SPECIAL REPORT series devoted to urine in accordance with the broadcasting code of ethics to be educational, inspirational, and entertaining. The first episode is on *Crisfeld's Encyclopedia*. *Urine*: waste material secreted by the kidneys in mammals and discharged as a slightly amber fluid. *Urinator*: one who urinates. *Urinous*: relating to, or having the qualities of urine.

Enuresis: the unintentional and involuntary loss of urine, referenced as early as Egyptian medical texts (1550 B.C.). *Auresis*: the inability to empty urine from the bladder. *Uromancy*: also known as *uroscopy*; the medieval medical practice of examining urine to forecast the future. *Uromancesis*: a pseudoscientific and alchemical analysis of urine pioneered by Lazaro Spallanzani in *De Urinis* (1687). *Urology*: the professional study of urine. *Uranus*: a planet in the solar system. No linguistic relation. In the library parking lot, carefully torn pages from the violated books clipped to clothesline will flutter in the breeze.

Expect one of the laid off factory workers, Moses Hamblin, to pace the room all night with his sick child. It will be the croup. Mr. Hamblin will rub ointment on the child's chest. He will remove the child's clothes and his own shirt believing skin to skin warmth will ease the child's breathing. Mr. Hamblin will tire. He will fall asleep. He will awake to silence. The child will no longer be wheezing, not even breathing. Its skin will be grayish blue. Mr. Hamblin will shake the child until it cries, until in a violent spasm it wets itself out of fear. Covered in urine, Mr. Hamblin will choke out sobs, hugging the child closer to his naked chest.

NOVEMBER

Expect unseasonal temperatures after 5 November. Expect the absence of muses, but do not fear. The impending solstice will bring disappointment followed by euphoria, but not before. Jupiter will be the ruling planet. The Archer will track his prey. Live recklessly, but avoid music in the key of C minor, marital relations, and decapitated chickens. Ignore the anniversary of the Soviet Union's collapse—it has no bearing on the outcomes of this year. Lucky numbers: 6, 31, 57, 78.

Expect to find an orange biohazard sticker smeared over Mr. Waldrep's car windshield. This will be part of a public health initiative to identify spaces marked by the urinator. In the evening, children will line up in a driveway and run to the car, touch the sticker, and run back to the driveway. The last child to return will be kicked to the ground. This will be the game.

Expect a **SPECIAL REPORT** on the Roman poet Catullus who rinsed his mouth with urine four times a day. He wrote 1,300 poems and fathered eighteen children.

Expect Wilbur Baum to sit in the basement listening to the radio static. He will sketch facial composites of what the urinator might look like. He will imagine him a scrawny specimen with eyes set deep in the face like an owl. He will imagine him with a pug nose and double chin. He will imagine him bearded with horn-rimmed glasses. There are those who will say the urinator is the kind of man who lives with his mother, the kind of man who doesn't believe in God, the kind of man who parks his car out in front of elementary schools, the kind of man who drinks alone in bars, but Wilbur Baum will always draw him smiling. He will hear on the radio about an emaciated Kitty Nielsen being carried out of the factory, the door padlocked behind her. Delirious, she will later tell the *Tribune* she couldn't believe the parking lot was full of weeds and broken glass and so strangely quiet. What happened to all the people?

she will ask dreamily. Come to bed, Wilbur, his wife will say from the top of the stairs.

Expect Mrs. Kimball to serve her famous lasagna. Seeing the yellow film on the bottom of the ceramic dish she will make a strange noise. It's just olive oil, Mr. Kimball will say. Mrs. Kimball will almost hyperventilate. It's just olive oil, Mr. Kimball will say again, serving himself a spoonful and putting it in his mouth. Mrs. Kimball will hurry the children into the street, screaming dreamily, almost happily, *We're infected!* Mr. Kimball will stay inside, chewing slowly, muttering, *This town, this goddamned town.*

Expect local news broadcasts to contain thirty seconds of updates on the factory strike, followed by nineteen minutes of urine-centric SPECIAL REPORTS interspersed with forty-one minutes of pharmaceutical advertisements for how to cure erectile dysfunction and hemorrhoids.

Expect Mrs. Jocelyn Thayer to visit the clinic. Looks normal, the doctor will say, examining her foot. It aches, Mrs. Thayer will say. You're getting older, the doctor will say. You don't understand, Mrs. Thayer will insist, whenever it aches I know things. Like the weather. Like how people are feeling. If someone nearby is sad, Mrs. Thayer will say, the pinky toe will get icy. Pain is a medical mystery, the doctor will shrug. Perhaps I'm infected, Mrs. Thayer will say. There is no infection, the doctor will say. But Mrs. Thayer will insist. She will say she was one of the swimmers in the aerobics class the day the pool closed down. I think I know where the urinator will strike next, she will say. It will take much restraint for the doctor not to tell her she suffers from delusions and if she persists she will twist deeper and deeper into herself like origami that longs to be a shape other than what it is, but that is not an acceptable medical diagnosis.

Expect a SPECIAL REPORT on the dyers of Yorkshire, many of whom had been banished from the Worshipful Company of Dyers in London for malfeasance, who were the most famous in the medieval world. Pope Clement VI had all his vestments dyed there. Ten thousand gallons of urine arrived secretly in the Yorkshire ports every month, used to make mordants to preserve coloring.

Expect the Elks Lodge will host the third annual Moustache Festival. Two nights before the opening ceremonies, a man will climb a ladder to adjust the marquee. Over the sign WELCOME FACIAL HAIR ENTHUSIASTS! he will spread a bright orange biohazard sticker.

Expect Wilbur Baum to stand in his driveway. He will stare at his map of the town with its yellow highlighting and push pins marking every appearance of the urinator. The map will not say whether this is terrorism or art or something else entirely. Outside, Wilbur Baum will stare at the stars. For the first time they will appear like holes cut out of a vast black tapestry, the light leaking through, and Wilbur Baum will remember his middle school science teacher who said there is no sound in space, and yet the stars make music when they die. Wilbur Baum will lie on his back, the grass itching his ears, wondering if the stars and the yellow highlights create a constellation. He will feel this incredible pressure against the inside of his head, as if that too is beginning to leak.

Expect the authorities to apprehend a suspect. His name will be Heber C. Hazlitt. Mr. Hazlitt will sign a confession. Charges of criminal malice will be filed. The more serious charge of conspiracy to incite public imagination will be pending. Co-workers at the factory will say Mr. Hazlitt exhibited a certain amphibian misanthropy. Wilbur Baum will welcome the news of Mr. Hazlitt's arrest with a frustrated joy. The urinator appeared with such banality but also much promise. There will be a crushing sadness in seeing a photograph of him. Wilbur Baum, like so many of his friends and neighbors, will prefer the rumor of him.

Expect sunrise at 7:21 A.M. and sunset at 6:14 P.M.

Expect the police will evacuate the tent city, telling the *Tribune* conditions were highly unsanitary.

Expect the cost of advertisements during the nightly news SPECIAL REPORTS to increase 400%.

Expect Lavinia Baum to prepare lamb chops, rare, the fastest way to a man's heart. She will light scented candles and open a bottle of apple cider they've been saving. Wilbur Baum will stay in the basement with his sketchpad. He will not be sure what he wants from the urinator, just as he does not know why he pins these sketches to the walls, or why he has maps of the town charting the urinator's attacks scattered on the floor. He only knows he must. Perhaps he will wish it is not too late to be marked, not with a biohazard sticker on his door, or even a toilet full of urine, but an inner mark, a quiet space opening inside him that feels inexplicable and lovely and not quite. He will turn up the radio.

Expect a waitress cleaning a table to find a prosthetic arm. She will tell nobody. The first three days she will keep it under the counter, expecting the owner to return to the café to retrieve his missing limb. She will imagine him tall with stubble. By the end of the week, she will be having breakfast with the prosthetic arm and tell it all about her day. She will practice dancing with the prosthetic arm for when the mystery man invites her to go dancing, to go for a long walk under the waning moonlight. After a double shift she will come home and rest her feet in the prosthetic hand's embrace, imagining what a massage might feel like. She will invite it into her bed. She will worry about it alone in the apartment. While waiting for the bus one night she will be seized by the fear of dying alone. As the bus is coming to a stop, she will inexplicably reach out to touch it, saved at the last minute by what she can only call a Good Samaritan. Returning home, she will be horrified to discover the prosthesis lodged in the bathroom toilet. She will admit to authorities she always intended to return the prosthesis to its rightful owner, but she was waiting. For what? The right moment. All these years, she will say, she felt something was missing, like she was born in the wrong time and in the wrong place, but with the prosthetic arm she felt rounded, smooth as a marble. She will weep seeing the prosthesis removed from the scene of the crime. Why would someone do such a strange thing? she will sob. Why?

Expect Wilbur Baum to substitute his face for the urinator's on flyers. **WANTED FOR QUESTIONING** in big letters at the top. He will spend the night stapling photocopies to lampposts.

Expect Mrs. Lucroy, a first-year teacher who will spend all afternoon daydreaming of retirement, to inspect Billy Havermann's desk before leaving the classroom. She will find three pencils, a turtle shell, two small incendiary devices, and a damp notebook. Opening the notebook, she will discover a graphic love note written to her, Mrs. Lucroy, with questionable illustrations. She will bring wet fingertips to her nose and just as her heart falls out of sync with the rest of her, across town expect Wilbur Baum to wait patiently in his office for the bathroom occupant to finish. It is the only office he will ever know. He will always feel it was an insult putting him next to the bathroom, a joke orchestrated by detectives who say his sketches are not realistic enough, that they ruined the investigation. For more than thirty years he has listened to people use the toilet and knows whose tinkling is like the night's sky and whose is a bulldozer, and who whistles and who recites Shakespearean sonnets. He will walk briskly inside the bathroom and lock the door. While kneeling to wipe up a few stray droplets he will remember when he was a child and went with his father to visit some people from church. A religious errand, his father called it, and he warned little Wilbur strange things might happen while they were praying at this house. The walls might bleed, his father said. Expect furniture to fly. Expect mists of darkness, imps, and weeping and wailing and gnashing of teeth from those spirits on the other side of the veil. After the prayer, when his father put a trembling hand around him and asked, *Did you feel that?* little Wilbur nodded slowly, not knowing how to tell him nothing happened, wetting himself right there in the car because he knew there wasn't any God. Kneeling on the bathroom tile Wilbur Baum will want to believe in prayer, will wish he was like his father who could make something out of nothing, will wish his mind was touched by the finger of God and could sketch the face of the urinator, but his words will be dull things, like static, filling the room with silence as he waits to feel something, to feel anything.

Expect Wilbur Baum to arrive at the church and find the doors locked. There will be no orange biohazard sticker, but there will be a handwritten note: SERVICES CANCELED. PLEASE CONSULT SPECIAL REPORT. GOD BLESS.

Expect distress, expect enthusiasm, when Mr. Hazlitt's urine sample will come back negative. Mr. Hazlitt will be escorted out of town by the sheriff. Not for criminal mischief, but for being an impostor.

Expect Wilbur Baum will give away the ham radio to an antique shop downtown and walk six blocks to the bistro where he will doodle on a napkin while his wife studies the menu without looking at him, remembering their second date, no, the sixth, when they stayed up late on her nicotine-stained sofa, bodies scissored, saying words just to say words, words about nothing, about nonsense, about God, words just to keep each other awake because the morning was uncertain and Wilbur Baum worried that if the words stopped she would crumble into a foreign alphabet, maybe Russian, and he wouldn't know how to make the sentence of her, and then sprawled out on the floor, ravenous, feeding each other handfuls of spaghetti because the silverware had gone missing, that yolk of a sun cracking through the horizon, the marinara dripping from her chin just as it will be at the bistro, and stuffing her mouth with noodles he asked her to marry him, her tongue licking wine dark teeth, and then her lips moving, just like they will be at the bistro when she will say, Your mustache looks nice, her voice faraway, like soft but electrifying static. He will rub the mustache with two fingers, imagining himself like a cowboy in a black and white western, then take a bite of salad and rub it again. It is lovely, he will think. It is lovely. It is.

Every Nerve Singing

After Julio Cortazar

Nobody believes me when I tell them how I became a jellyfish. It's no mystery. It happened years ago. Maybe centuries. I don't remember. Time is measured differently for jellies. We are invertebrates. You'd be surprised how senseless a spine can make you.

There was a travelling science exhibit. Twice a year they rented a gray brick building on South Temple not far from Brigham Young's old Beehive House. Once they displayed a unicorn tusk. Another year they promised a mermaid but really it was a large fish tail sewn together with a monkey suspended in formaldehyde. I saw it eleven times. The year I discovered the jellyfish was the year with the exhibit of Einstein's brain. The picture on the flyer looked like pasta.

I was the first in line. The paper wasp nests were sad and the bezoars and thousand-year-old egg seemed fake. My father's bookkeeper followed me room to room, whispering inane things until I lost him in the room with a floating light bulb. The Chinese acupuncture needles were boring and the pickled homunculus in the jar looked asleep. I didn't expect to enjoy the jellyfish but found myself watching them for hours.

The next morning, I returned. The jellyfish exhibit was in a small room on the fourth floor. A black curtain hung in the doorway. *Medusozoa*, the plaque said. The only light behind the curtain came from the pinks and blues and lavenders radiating from the jellyfish bodies floating inside an enormous aquarium tank. I lost count of them. Some were like disks of alien moons, while others fanned their tentacles in great swaths of golden hair like decapitated Rapunzels. They pulsed from one end of the tank to the other, lost in their aimlessness. I tapped on the glass. They ignored me. One was shaped like a church bell. It pulsed gently, a long bridal veil of tentacles in its wake. As it passed in its loop, I thought I heard music.

In the hallway I leaned against a doorway. It hurt to breathe, like all the air had been sucked out of the sky. Such a waste, yes? a voice behind me said. It was my father's friend, the bookkeeper. He was thin and boyish with hair that looked as if his mother had combed it.

We walked around the fountain. The bookkeeper talked about Einstein's brain and assured me on the scale of marvelous things it was a zero. He was fond of zeroes. Zero is the happiest of numbers, he told me. At the end of the day, if a man can go home to a fat wife and fall asleep with a full stomach and zeroes in his ledger, well, that is a happy man, the bookkeeper smiled.

We slept together. Don't be so surprised. After being in the presence of the jellyfish I needed to wrap myself around something warm and useless like a man.

In the morning, unable to think of anything else all night, I crept out of the room and bought a ticket to see the jellyfish again.

Nobody else came to see the jellies. Their movements paralyzed me. One by one they circled the tank like luminescent gorgons. They took no notice of me, and yet I knew they were aware of me. Their only imperative was to float. Spinelessness had set them free. I was mesmerized by their tentacles, oblivious to the world yet stretched blindly as if hoping to be embraced. Despite their blindness their tentacles only rarely tangled as they circled the tank and when they did twist together it was a kiss of sorts, their gelatinous bodies never twisting in awkward revulsion from one another the way people do on a crowded street. The more I watched the more I attuned to their secret desire to exist outside of time, that is, to live sideways, which is why we jellies are seldom vertical or horizontal but always floating at an angle.

Once, I gathered up the courage and pressed my palm to the glass. Dozens of jellies floated toward me. Their protoplasmic bodies brushed against the glass and, for a moment, the world turned inside-out, like when you're staring at your reflection in the spoon and one of your teeth aches but you're not sure if it's you or the reflection.

I returned again and again to the exhibit, arriving early in the morning and staying until late at night. There was an unspeakable sadness to the jellyfish tentacles that filled me with joy. I could only imagine what it must be like having a billion nerves coiled around something no thicker than a thread of silk. What a frenzy of feeling. So why did I pity them? Was it because of how fragile their bodies were? How easily they disintegrated, leaving only a lavender glow in their wake? Before the jellies I had always believed things should be long or fragile but not both, but I began to wonder if I was mistaken and to be soft and delicate was what it meant to be alive.

Then I would go home and crawl into bed with the bookkeeper who flowered me with affections, feeding me green

Jell-O with his fingers and counting the number of kisses he doled out, as if he wished to own me in his mouth. But as the weeks turned into months, I no longer felt him floating inside me late at night because as soon as the lights were out I sensed nothing except the jellyfish songs.

I'm not sick. Jellyfish, I discovered on a radio program, are accomplished musicians, although their sounds exist outside the frequencies of what humans can hear. I was watching the curator feed the jellyfish one evening when I heard something deep within my ear. It was a Sunday. I remember wearing my mother's blue dress. The curator climbed a wobbly ladder and opened the tank. She scooped her hand into a bucket and spread almost invisible droplets into the water. The jellies danced. That's when I heard it. A ripple, or a murmur, or a hum. Like when a spoon makes that tingling sound stirring a tea cup. I didn't realize until then that the jellies had been singing all this time. It was an old song, chanted in the beginning before there were earths or stars and all was protoplasmic soup.

One night I combed the tangles from my hair at the mirror. The bookkeeper was sleeping in the other room. I hummed the queer jellyfish melody, bringing the hair against my lips until they tingled with an odd burning sensation.

And then I knew. I was becoming a jellyfish.

I did what any normal person would do. I bought a ticket and went straight to the jellyfish exhibit. I undressed. Opening the hatch, I slipped inside the aquarium tank.

I floated. The bloom welcomed me into their elliptical swirl. My hair began to glow but my skin was stubbornly opaque. There was music everywhere. The shapes of two girls materialized on the other side of the glass. I floated towards them. They wore prim dresses and shiny shoes. One look at me and they screamed.

Suddenly, two burly men hooked me under the armpits and hoisted me out the tank. The other jellyfish shrieked. They cried. They lighted up the room with their fluorescence. If only the men had waited a few more seconds the transformation would have been complete. Then nobody would have confused me for a girl. But out I came, nude as a moon, flopping on the ground. I coughed up water. A crowd huddled over me. Someone slapped me on the back trying to help me breathe. It felt as if I were still floating, my head spinning with music. I tried to talk but my voice was burnt. Before anyone said anything, I fled down the stairs and into the night.

I spent hours in the marina. I studied my reflection in the water. I was still a girl, but not quite a girl. My skin was pale, my hair a beautiful tangle. And yet these limbs. This voice. Breathing this rancid air. What to do with myself? Nobody wants a not quite girl.

They found me the next morning in a fisherman's boat. They said they had been looking for me all night and I was lucky the fisherman found me, almost mistaking me for seaweed.

At the hospital they wrapped me in blankets and tried to force warm soups down my throat. I vomited. Cold, I told them, give me something cold. The nurse didn't believe me when I told her I was a jellyfish and needed to get back to the water before I dried out.

My father was the only visitor. He was so small and shriveled, like a raisin left in the sun. He stopped in the doorway, startled, as if he'd stumbled into someone else's dream. I could tell it pained him when I refused to hug him.

A jellyfish sting can be toxic, I said. You believe me, don't you?

Oh poppet, my father mumbled. Then he ran his fingertips over the top of my head as if confused who I was.

I told him we had to hurry, that there was no time, that I needed to get back to the exhibit, back to my bloom, that I was almost a jellyfish and without water I would disintegrate into a gelatinous blob, but he kept whispering poppet, poppet, and kissed my forehead. It tingled.

Nobody else believed me either. Don't be absurd, a man at the park said, pushing me aside with his cane when I asked if my hair looked like tentacles. Good God, a young father said, hurrying away with his child when I asked him to touch me to see if I would sting.

Nobody would tell me what I was. The more I thought about it, the more they told me it never happened. The less they believed me the more I knew what I was. I was a jellyfish. A half jellyfish, anyway. The more I believed this, the more it made me ache. My hair fell out. My skin wrinkled and was always damp. Burning up one minute and freezing the next. I lost a tooth.

Why are you so anxious? the doctor asked during a routine check-up, as if that explained what was happening to me.

Wouldn't you be anxious if you were a jellyfish? Wouldn't you be anxious if you were shedding this wretched human skin for something immortal?

I see, he scribbled in his notebook.

To speak to a doctor of immortality is a foolish thing. Of course he wouldn't understand that we jellyfish are immortal. I read about it in the library book. No, we don't live forever. But we can, when necessary, turn back the clock. We mature backwards. Our tentacles retract, our bodies collapse, shrinking back into infantile shapes, we sink to the ocean floor and start life all over again as little polyps.

Before I was a jellyfish, when I had a spine and laughter and menstruation, I thought of living as a straight line with God waiting at the far end with a cudgel. But with the jellies I've come to realize we are not hurling relentlessly towards zero, but this life is one among many, a web spun at many angles and when one strand breaks another spins unexpectedly to take its place.

One night I drew a bath and turned off all the lights. I scratched and clawed and gnawed at my skin, but skin is a stubborn thing. Nobody knows this, but when you finally peel through enough human skin there is bioluminescence. Most people stop when they draw blood. They stop before they get to the greens and blues. They're afraid to see what's inside them.

Soon my skin was as pale as lemons sucked free of their juices. What else could I do? The more I peeled away the more my skin burned with song.

Now I sit in my bathtub all day, waiting for this skin to shed. Soon I will no longer be this half-jellied thing in a human cage. Soon I will disintegrate into a polyp, sucked down the drain and flushed out into rivers and lakes as I mature back into childhood. Like my sisters, I am immortal. I can only guess what my next life will be.

I am eaten by a sea turtle.

I am caught in a biologist's net. He takes me to his laboratory where, after many experiments, he transdifferentiates my cells and I assume a human shape so I can join him at the marine biology gala. After midnight I turn back into a jellyfish and the scientist weeps.

I am put into a vat with a thousand other jellies and we are boiled into syrup and sold to elderly women who rub us all over their buttocks hoping to smooth away their wrinkles.

I am floating alone and free in the restless ocean.

I am dissected in a high school laboratory. One boy steals a tentacle and later, with his friends, plays a game seeing who can keep my tentacle down their underwear the longest.

I am scooped out of a tide pool by the survivor of some nuclear catastrophe and he draws pictures of me on cave walls.

I am pickled and sprinkled over a bed of jasmine rice in a restaurant.

I am the pet of a fisherman's wife. She keeps me in a salt pool cave where we sing to each other and share dirty jokes. Our laughter surprises the stars.

I am swallowed up in a black hole with the rest of the universe. All is silent and dark until I start to pulse, to sing, to shine, and the cosmos is reborn.

I am floating in an aquarium, singing for a girl who presses her face close to the glass, as if she can hear our song.

I am washed ashore on an abandoned beach. A mustachioed man spears me with a stick. He laughs, tosses me into a clump of seaweed. A boy chases a girl across the sand. You are Rapunzel and I am the prince, he says. He tries to kiss her. The girl, skinny as a weed with frizzy hair, grabs me by the tentacles and swings my serpentine blob at him again and again, paralyzing the poor brute with her fearsomeness. Even after the boy sulks away the girl doesn't let go of me. I am on fire. Every nerve singing. But the girl doesn't let go. Her hand is purpled and numb and she can't tell where she ends and I begin and yet she fists me, gently, her flesh singing, screaming, blooming, no longer a foolish little girl but a woman, astonished nobody told her this is kissing.

The Kind of Invisible You Are

It was Fat Jim who told the Sunday school girls about the no-nos. He told us about the Russians and Gaylord Perry's spitball and that widower from Ogden with the alien crop circles in his chest hair, but all we cared about were the no-nos. Everybody loved Fat Jim. Slick as a saint. Shook hands with the prophet twice. And the minty aftershave? And that choir voice like gravel spilled in a bucket? Oof. He owned four-hundred and eighty-seven lambs and knew them all by name. Sometimes I think about Fat Jim doing it to her at the old dream mine just past Pond Town. He takes her by the hand down into the mine shaft and I can't see Sissy's face getting red, but I can hear her voice swallowed up by the dark. Must've been a month before the neighbor finally told dad what happened.

Some bad luck, dad said, for all of us.

The mouth on you, I said.

Next thing you know she'll gone stray, dad said after a long quiet. He was a fool, but what do you expect from a man with seven daughters who'd left home and never looked back? Sissy and I were the last two. He was a fool, but he was our fool.

Nobody said a thing to Fat Jim. During the week he was just another farmer but on Sundays he became Brother Jim bringing in pictures of the no-nos. Little stick figure boys and girls with square faces. We all laughed. Square faces! Every week we lined up for Sunday school like little angels in dresses and suits and begged: *Tell us again, brother Jim. Tell us about the no-nos.* Then he'd settle in his chair and take off his glasses and pull in a handful of gut and sort of lean back with his eyes closed, teeth poking through his lips like a beaver: Once there was a little girl who always said no, he'd say. She loved the word. But then she started saying it everywhere. When she said it, her face turned red and twisted up like a knot. If you're not careful your face will get stuck that way, her father told her. But she didn't listen.

Everyone but Sissy took turns going into the bathroom and turning off all the lights and whispering no, no, no, but nobody's face got stuck.

Dad kept Sissy on the farm hoping she wouldn't gone stray. All the church girls were teasing her about being a merry-go-round and wondering if she'd sell tickets cheap so they didn't have to. Girls are assholes, dad said, and gave her some of mom's old jewelry.

You'd think the business with Fat Jim would make a girl go dark, but it turned Sissy right holy. No more sneaking cigarettes on the roof. No more gone stray to the old airport hangar where the mechanics were all too happy to lick up the Petri dish of her. No more scratching anarchy symbols on her thighs with paperclips. She got the dolphin tattoo on her wrist removed and stopped wearing all the piercings, even the cute belly button one. Took to wearing creamy floor-length dresses and pinching her hair up in a bun, even praying at the dinner table until the food went cold. Weird Provo girls started coming by the house. Sinewy and pale like vampires escaped from some movie set. They read scripture to the sheep. They did baptisms for the dead. They hugged strangers on the bus. They put on roller skates and sang hymns while skitching on the back of RVs and pickup trucks. Once, Sissy showed me the road rash on her elbow after a car swerved and she did a few somersaults on the asphalt. Her arms were bony, the veins beneath her skin latticed like spider webs. The scab looked a little like Jesus, or at least a better Jesus than the one Sariah Yorgensen found on the potato chip last year.

But I knew she wasn't all holy. I knew about the penknife she kept tucked into a fold of her dress. Just in case, she once told me.

Sissy warned me that if I wasn't careful the no-nos would come take me away to no man's land. I set a trap outside the window just in case, but instead of a no-no it caught a jackalope. Before it died it told my mother to divorce dad because he was a liar and a cheat. She's been gone stray ever since.

Wasn't long before Sissy was having visions of the dream mine. The one brother Koyle started digging half a century ago because an angel told him to. You can see it coming around the south bend of Highway 89, a pale concrete bunker gnawing out of the mountain like a ragged tooth. Everybody's heard the story. The mine full of gold that will save we believers when the catastrophe comes. Never mind nobody's found even a speck of gold yet. Hardly a man in Utah doesn't own a few shares. Dad keeps his under his pillow along with a pistol.

After a night of singing hymns outside the mine shaft with the Provo girls, Sissy would come home and eat bowls of frogeye salad dad made just for her. When he asked what she'd seen she'd smile and say, It's coming up angels, as if that was supposed to mean something. When dad fell asleep watching TV, we'd climb out the window like old times and follow the arroyo to the fence and press our faces against the chain link and look past the airplane hangar, look west over the Oquirrh mountains where they buried the uranium and on some nights the haze evaporating off the waste pool rose like incense from Solomon's temple. They say the yellowcake slurry will still be wasting away like a neon opera ten million years from now, Sissy said. You think we'll still be sisters then? I didn't say anything. We sat there as time turned into a jellyfish pulsing gooey trails of light.

One Sunday, Sissy came home crying after the church girls said maybe if she let Fat Jim do it to her again she'd go back to being a virgin and then she could have a baby in the desert and start a new religion. After that, Sissy couldn't stop talking babies. They're in heaven, she'd say, just spirits now waiting for me to grow them a body. She taught them their ABCs and they followed her around the house all day crying up something awful and refusing to potty train. When she wasn't mopping invisible heavenly piss off the floor she sang them hymns and told them about the no-nos. Dad was happy when Sissy found a job at the Big H, thinking serving up burgers might keep her from gone stray, but the sheriff brought her home a few hours later when a customer complained she threatened to slit their throats because meat is murder. She locked herself in the room and doodled more pictures of the no-nos before using mom's old bottle of perfume to set them on fire.

Dad got her some good pills after that. When she woke up, he tried to drag her to church but she said she was Zoroastrian now. Last night, she said, she'd hopped the military fence and wandered into a bunker where men in hazmat suits engineered sex-crazed mosquitoes. Everyone bitten will fuck each other to death in a giant orgy to hasten the coming of the goddess Anahita. They'll call it rapturitis, she said. She spent the rest of the day staring out the window at mom's old bicycle collecting rust.

Poor Sissy. Like so many girls in Utah her head was full of words, but she just couldn't give birth to the story of herself.

Girls are just star stuff to boys, Sissy said in her faraway voice. Like constellations. See there? she said, pointing at the sky, like the Pleiades. Six sisters and the one gone stray at the end. Like me. But, she said, getting real close to whisper in my ear, don't forget the stars fucking burn. She told me how when everything is destroyed it would be Anahita, the fertile one, the mighty of waters, who would stand in the cosmic rubble and put the world back together atom by atom. Anahita who would decide what kind of invisible you are. Then she took me to the dream mine. Traced my finger along the chewed-up sign hanging from the gate with a picture of skull and crossbones and POISON written in big letters. I tried to picture Fat Jim doing it to me and whether my face would twist into a no-no knot or if I'd look down the mine shaft and pray for angels too. Not the fragile ones you see in all that Michelangelo bullshit. No robes, which are bad for warfare. These angels will be naked, their tits bouncing in the wind and their well-oiled muscles steaming from residual celestial heat. Eyes like glittering diamonds. White wings spackled with gore. Nobody knows what's down the mine shafts. Most of it flooded now, but the scientists say there's probably enough uranium to make our bones fluorescent for a thousand years. Lord, it's a strange thing to mine dreams.

The next morning, the sheep were all missing. Sissy too. Gone stray, dad said.

It was Fat Jim who said he saw them heading west toward Skull Valley. When we got there, it was a cataclysm of sheep. White patches in the sagebrush as far as you could see, like clouds fallen out of the sky. Some dead, some paralyzed, some twitching like they were filled with the Holy Spirit. Others vomiting blood and bile, bleating, wheezing, dizzying, choking on the air, eyes gone green, lips searching for sounds in the ancient ovine alphabet to describe their misery.

It was all over the news. Army disposing of thousands of barrels of VX gas, they said, but everyone knew it was just another sign of the times. Maybe we should have seen it coming. That's what this Utah is, isn't it? Misfits, perverts, and prophets all swept up by apocalyptic fever. In Armageddon we trust. All my sisters have gone stray. Still, I can't quit it.

The sheep faces looked pickled, their eyes swollen shut. Maybe that was for their sake. Or mine. I try not to think about it. Fat Jim was trembling. His babies were all dead. He whispered their names. He said it hurt to breathe, like something invisible was drumming away on his lungs with an ice pick.

I sat next to one of the ewes in the ditch. Her mouth was frothy green. Her eyes were glazed and she was still breathing as a Gila monster gnawed on her lambing hole. I'd never seen anything like it before. The penknife was in my hand. I could have slit her throat. I could have slit all their throats. Only I didn't.

Mrs. Gila monster hissed at me, flicked her tongue at the air. A real sassy bitch. Sissy and I used to throw rocks at them. Some Indians say when you see a Gila monster you should run. Her venom can kill a horse. Other Indians say her bite will heal any disease. But you never know what it will be, poison or cure, until you're bitten. That's the way with everything.

I closed my eyes and tried to think about Khrushchev and nuclear proliferation and that yellowcake slurry steaming on the other side of the mountain and for a moment it was like God and I were both breathing enriched uranium. Salty wind licked my face.

When I opened my eyes Mrs. Gila monster had stopped gnawing on the lamb and was looking at me with the dead lights in her eyes. I felt her voice inside me. Do you like those fingers? They're clumsy with boys, but would you like me to take them? Or what about your face? It's shaped like your mother's. How about I take a little nibble off that cheek? Or that stubborn fat around your belly? Will you miss that? Or that ear? The one your dad promised to get pierced but by the time he came home from church it was too late so Sissy stopped by the store for safety pins and a lighter. Aren't you tired of listening to everyone else? You've had it long enough. How about I take that ear?

Yes, I whispered. Yes, yes, yes.

The Abridged Recipes of St. Marguerite for Fevers, Chills, Visions, and Other Marital Ailments

Find a man at the speed-dating convention, preferably one with an appetite, and suck his cock in the janitor's closet after eating a peanut butter sandwich, pretending not to remember his allergy. Halleluiah, he will whisper as his skin breaks out in hives.

———————

He is your second husband, a soon-to-be Mormon bishop, always putting things in his mouth. Grass. Pennies. Baklava. When visiting friends, he never fails to lick their wallpaper. It's repulsive, but after telling you he kept a pet butterfly under his tongue as a boy you just have to kiss him. On the night he proposes, you roam Main Street. Nervous, he stuffs his mouth with rocky mountain oysters and green Jell-O. He can't remember anything, he claims, if he doesn't put it in his mouth. Mom took me to all kinds of doctors, he shrugs, but my mouth has a case of the swallows. A tongue beyond science, he smiles, an insatiable thing.

He isn't the first Mormon boy sweet on your skin. Is it true you're one of Cain's granddaughters? they laughed at church. Then you'd look them in the eye and they'd grin. Or do you look like caramel because you swallow? they said. Such desert boys. Soft and stupid. Marshmallows playing with fire hoping to get burned. That's the only kind of boy out here in Utah. Boys who think they become immortal by making others feel invisible. Boys who hope you are the cane to stain their tongues. Frida, Frida, Frida, they whisper. They think it means fried. Really, it means peace. But you can be a fried thing too.

When the power goes out, spoon him tapenade as he reads Leviticus. Later, let him suck olive juice off your nipples, never admitting you plucked them from a can left half-opened last summer, the juices sexing with botulism.

While he sleeps caress his throat, secretly measuring the width of his windpipe with your fingertips, because tomorrow you will make ricotta cavatappi and there will be a perfect cherry tomato to wedge inside there.

At breakfast, spread homemade yew berry jam over his toast and pretend he is paranoid when he complains of trembling hands and blurry vision.

Bring home a Himalayan salt lick. Tell him to give one lick before every meal to prime the taste buds. Then, months later, once he is no better than Pavlov's dog, stop cooking with salt. Make him beg. When the only flavor comes from licking your skin, then you know he is already dead.

Take him with you to pick cucumbers. No, too small, you say. Too many blemishes, you say. Too fat. Too crooked. That reminds me, you start to say, then shake your head and do that thing with your hair he likes. As you scrub cucumbers in the sink, remind him of the boy who took your virginity. As you prepare the brine, remind him of the boy you left at the altar. As you snap one between your teeth, spitting out the cucumber juice, remind him of the husband before him. Watch the color drain from his face. Watch him bite his lip with wonder. Seduce him with doubt and murder him with imagination.

For his birthday, bake a layered chocolate cake glazed in fondant and topped with pink oleanders. Assure him the flowers are edible. It will take six days for the toxins to work their magic, his body will expel juices that pool on the floor and evaporate into a pink perfume.

———

Go mushroom foraging. Bake him a galette with Swiss chard. When the first seizure comes, assure him he's just laughing too hard. When you open his wrist with the dull edge of a pie cutter, persuade him the mushrooms must have been hallucinogenic and he will lap up his own blood like syrup on pancakes.

———

Feed him angel hair pasta. Combing fingers through your hair he will believe you are his angel. Leave a Hansel and Gretel trail of wet pasta noodles on the stairs as he licks Alfredo sauce off your fine harp of ribs. After, ask him to get you a glass of water. His heels are weak, and he will slip going down the stairs, even if he needs some gentle encouragement.

———

Bake an apple pie. His mother's recipe, the one she made after the neighbor boys teased him. Add three extra teaspoons of cinnamon. Later, when his tongue pauses gliding over your asshole to scrape the cinnamon clumps from his molars, the wires in his brain will scramble as he confuses you for his mother. An aneurysm is inevitable.

———

You don't meet his mother until after you're married. On Sundays, they busy themselves in the kitchen, just the two of them, lost in a perfume of saffron and nutmeg, chittering in some strange speak. Cinnamon flakes from her bird's nest of hair onto the countertop and more than once you catch him dabbing it with a finger and licking indiscreetly. You never have a meal quite like mother, he smiles, taking her hand to say grace. Later, in the dark of his childhood room, his fat tongue traces your hips, your ribs, like it is a picnic and you the rack of lamb.

———————

When he phones late you smell ginger, clove, deceit in his voices. I'm with mother, he says, don't wait up. But warm the leftovers.

———————

The great Italian chef Martino di Como, who wrote a recipe for kangaroo brains, says soup is the only way to a man's soul.

———————

Cook with a vengeance, simmering down the beef bones with the viscera until it is gelatin. Strain the broth, simmer again. Sing hymns while skimming fat. About Calvary, about the virgin of the lake. Onions. Potatoes. Beets. Grated dill. It needs more flavor. Baptize it with a touch of phlegm. Three drops of pus from a blister on your knee. A trickle of piss. Watch an old bandage wilt like a basil sprig. Then earwax. Then bile. It needs salt. Add the old tampons saved under the sink. The body is an abyss. Bring to a boil.

Fuck, the boys say when they visit your kitchen. Fuck. Fuck. Fuck. And lick the bowls clean. Mmmm, don't you know curses taste good.

There is bleach under the sink. But your man is a man of God and needs something holy. With a spoon you scrape the blood between your thighs, the elemental you, stirred until the soup is a red, frothy swirl.

Taste a spoonful. Hot. Salty. If there is a soul, this is what it tastes like. Then another. Not a sip but a swallow, a sacrament. Licking drops off the floor, the soup pirouetting inside you like a caged ballerina. You wish you saved him a little of the abyss of you. You wish you saved him, a little. But you—you could not stop.

Colorless Green Ideas Sleep Furiously

The morning fog is thinning when Frank leaves the diner and sees gargoyles perched on telephone wires. They whisper in a weird raspy chatter, oblivious to the rain. From his pocket Frank produces a whistle, blowing gently. One of the gargoyles, its hairy balls dangling like old lemons, swoops down. It coos as it scuttles closer, flashing blood-stained teeth and filthy but impressive wings. Frank pets it with one hand while reaching into his pocket for the syringe. The other gargoyle flies away.

Frank sighs. It's the sixth case this morning. Already he's wrestled a boojum and fished a tie-dyed baby from a sewer. He was on his way to get coffee when walking through the park he intercepted a naked fat man with gold skin and nipple rings. Since when do people want the Buddha for an imaginary friend? The awakened one glanced furtively at Frank, laughed *Not today motherfucker!*, and started running. Frank Jinxed him under the tire swing.

A crowd on the other side of the yellow tape boos and hisses as the Sweepers decontaminate the playground. The rain is a steady drizzle.

You look awful, Veronica says. She slurps yellow noodles thin as worms from a takeout box. Her arms are ornamented with purple scars like Victorian wallpaper. Veronica's never seen a Buddha for a friendly, and neither had Frank until an hour ago. Cherubs, Yetis, and little green Martians, sure, but never a Buddha.

Buddhas can be real assholes, Veronica smiles.

Frank ignores her, eyes fixed on the stain spread over the sandbox. Like coils of white mist but greasy to the touch. Friendlies always leave behind that white shit. A cadet in the standard cream-colored jumpsuit is on his knees collecting the residue like an archeologist. Sweepers. What an asinine name for an agency responsible for policing the imaginary friend population. The fact of the matter is when a friendly gets Jinxed there's a sticky mess no sweeping can fix.

Frank? Veronica tugs at his arm.

Still here, he mumbles, staring at the greasy white mist.

Veronica offers him noodles, but he wrinkles his nose in disgust. Before she can ask any questions, or invite him to lunch, or her bed, or wherever it is she wants to go, Frank's GPS vibrates. He studies the coordinates on the faceplate. The Avenues. He's relieved when Veronica's GPS lights up too, her coordinates signaling across town.

Tag team? she asks.

Your teeth are stained, Frank says, leaving her standing in the rain as he cuts through the diner parking lot where a second team of sweepers decontaminates what's left of the gargoyle.

———

There are worse jobs, of course. Like the factory where they make the noodles. Frank shudders at the thought of that yellow waste spooling out of a machine, even if they seem to be the only thing holding him together these days. The pay is shit, but the work is mindless and that's precisely its appeal. Distracted. Numb. Maybe that's what created this mess in the first place. Too many people with too much imagination and nowhere to put it.

The first friendlies were unexpected. Psychological leftovers from childhood that somehow materialized in collective reality. You could touch them, hear them, smell them, play games with them, cry with them, fuck them if that's what you really wanted. There was nothing to fear, the scientists said. Pay your bills, mow your lawn. The world isn't ending, but it did just get a whole lot stranger.

Even Frank couldn't deny it was fun in the beginning. Who wouldn't want a reunion with an imaginary friend? Mermaids, clowns, alien blobs—people rekindled all kinds of nonsense from their childhood memories. Other times it was involuntary. Your mind wandered, your heart ached and *poof!*—an imaginary friend to keep you company. THIS IS THE END OF LONELINESS! the newspapers announced. Nobody believed that, but they all wanted to believe it would be the end of the way things used to be. There were naysayers, naturally. Always some group protesting, warning the friendlies were a plague, the result of a tainted water supply, or the pesticides, or electromagnetic waves—the punishment from God crowd surprisingly quiet—but none of that has never been proven.

Rounding the corner, Frank sees there's been another raid. From a church basement the Sweepers lead a hand-cuffed parade of friendlies into a transport destined for the facility where they'll be Jinxed back into nonexistence or wherever it is they go to die. Humanely, as the television PSAs always say.

The crowd here is more impressive than at the playground. Believers. Shit, Frank smirks. They hold signs and chant about preserving the imagination, how fake things have feelings too. Sometimes they throw bottles but mostly they fade into the blur that is this city. They sound like Frank's mother. She was a true-believing Mormon. Her ancestors pioneered across the plains until their feet bled, then conjured up angels to carry them the rest of the way. Why is the government so afraid of the invisible things in God's plan? she asked. Frank hadn't been to church since she died.

Hurrying past the crowd Frank sees a Sweeper standing over a chalky puddle of what used to be a friendly. He takes a photograph, probably for the wall back at the station.

Ronald Reagan, the sweeper smiles. Frank nods. There's an inordinate number of imaginary Ronald Reagans these days.

Already, Frank's regretting not tag-teaming with Veronica. She's a nice girl. Naïve but kind. Kindness goes a long way these days. He's tried to warn her about that, but she won't listen. If he asked, she'd comb his hair while telling her all the things he's seen, all the things he can't unsee, make him feel like he's not dangling on strings. He worries Veronica is not real at all, a figment of his imagination he conjured after his daughter died. Lately it scares him to talk with her. She thinks too much. Do friendlies feel anything when they're Jinxed? What if they're not gone at all, jus momentarily zeroed? Can you really zero a zero? Is it really killing if it's just an imaginary thing? Like will God send us to hell for what we do with our imaginations?

God is a friendly, Frank told her the other night.

Don't say that, Veronica whispered as if she was in church.

Frank misses nonsense. He used to hide in a little tent with a canopy of glow-in-the-dark stars playing a game with his daughter where they invented gibberish. *Emift. Woofsnitzel.* Or they would whisper nonsense things like *supernova with butterfly kisses.* Or *the gostak distims the doshes.* And *glocky kuzdra shteckly budled the bocker and kurdyaks the bockerling.* She stopped playing with him when her friendly appeared. Sometimes Frank still lies in the tent wondering if his breaths are real. Nine years with the Sweepers, and for what? It's like that whack-a-worm game in the old penny arcade. For every friendly Jinxed another two pop up somewhere else in the city. Never-ending work is good for the pocketbook but bad for the mind. Friendlies are inescapable these days: television, radio, billboards. For something so imaginary they certainly seem more real than the real.

News stations maintain a death toll. To set the public at ease, the mayor said. Frank often spends his nights downtown staring blankly at the neon electronic ticker outside the news station in disbelief of so many zeroes.

———

From the driveway she looks ordinary. A pale silhouette in a white dress leaning against the doorway, her twin braided tresses hanging to her hips like some Rapunzel. She's been waiting more than an hour but smiles as Frank comes up the steps, reaching out to shake his hand as if she's not annoyed in the least.

I'm here for the friendly, he says.

She offers him a drink and Frank declines, noticing the butter knife gripped in her scratched fingers, trembling, knuckles white as piano keys.

After the first few dozen friendlies made the news, the Mormon prophet got up at the pulpit and said it was a sign from God. No clue whether it was a catastrophe or a blessing. Just a sign, he said. Frank's come plenty of times to the Avenues to Jinx imaginary prophets.

Without a word, the woman in white leads him through the vaulted entryway with crystal chandeliers and up a maze of stairs and hallways where the woman loses her way once or twice before stopping outside the private bathroom. They stand there for a minute, her eyes shy but piercing, listening to the voice singing on the other side of the door.

It's in there, the woman says. Her voice is a little weird, a bit dazed like she's crawled out from a dream, but Frank knows rich people are usually nervous if not oblivious when it comes to friendlies. It can't be easy having all that leisure time to misunderstand the world. He presses his ear to the door.

She's a siren, that one, the woman says, almost hissing the words between her teeth. Better Jinx her before she talks you out of your own skin.

After nearly a decade on the job Frank is not surprised by such cruelty. People see friendlies as a nuisance, but for a certain type of person there's nothing more shameful than a friendly. It makes them feel less human. They're the savage kind that likes to watch the Jinxing. It's not pretty.

Frank blows on the whistle. The singing behind the door fades into a whisper. He whistles again. It's inaudible to humans, supposedly, because according to the scientists, imaginary things exist at a different frequency and are enticed by the sound. Veronica says she's heard it once. Impossible, Frank told her. No really, she smiled, like an echo inside an echo.

Does it have a name? Frank asks the woman.

Yumi. That's what I've always called her, the woman half-smiles, grinding her big toe into the carpet and avoiding looking at Frank. Silly, right? Don't you wish you could be a kid all over again?

Are you the host? Frank asks, scribbling on the report, not in the mood for mindless chit-chat. The woman looks away.

Wonderful, Frank thinks. A stowaway. Should have expected it in a gated community like the Avenues, oldest neighborhood in Salt Lake City. A leftover from childhood, probably. Hidden during the purges, kept a secret all these years. He can only wonder what's behind that door. Once Frank raided a factory and found fifty half-naked friendly stowaways chained up in shipping crates. There's an impressive black market for imaginary friends, the more exotic the better. The woman in white doesn't look like the type, but neither does she seem to be with the Believers who shuffle friendlies between safe houses. Of course, you can never really know someone.

And who can blame a woman like this for being unable to let go of childhood? After the wave of enthusiasm, relations with the friendlies soured quickly. Most were harmless, but one moldy apple can rot the bunch. There were incidents. Assaults. Impersonations. People started questioning what was real and what was fake. More than a few real people were purged, all in the name of preserving so-called traditional reality. By the time the government created the Bureau of Imagination and trained the first generation of Sweepers, things had gotten out of hand. Scientific testing in basements. Vigilante groups holding public executions of friendlies had to be curtailed. Martial law. Curfews. Barbaric tests to prove existence. For a time, there was an orphanage where imaginary friends were detained while the government decided what legal status they might have, but the extermination order was put into effect quickly.

I'm not a monster, the woman in white says suddenly, her eye twitching as she bites her lip to keep from crying. She's part of me, the woman says. Part of us. She's family, even if she isn't real. We couldn't just get rid of her, you know?

Frank can't argue with that. What else can you do with figments of your imagination, these pools of frustrated desire, except hold on?

———————

Frank locks the bathroom door behind him. After nine years he's seen just about everything. Friendlies made of moon dust. Friendlies who shit gold. One kid had a microscopic imaginary friend named Ray who lived inside the kid's mouth and had to be extracted with tweezers. Another friendly was an enormous ear. So, Frank's a little surprised to see a naked woman with dreadlocks stretched out in the empty tub. No tentacles, no fangs, no scales, no wings. Just a normal imaginary woman.

She keeps singing, ignoring him even when he sits on the edge of the bathtub. She keeps her eyes closed. Clever girl, Frank thinks. Friendlies have a nystagmus and the more they talk the more their pupils rattle around like marbles. It's one of the few ways to distinguish them from real people. There's nothing a friendly enjoys more than talking and the longer they talk the more excited they get and the faster they'll reveal what they really are.

If you're wondering, yes, the woman says, these tits are real.

Frank smiles. With everything so crazy now he often forgets the funny women in the world are usually imaginary.

She says your name is Yumi, Frank says after a long silence.

Hmmm. Is that what she says?

I'm just the Sweeper, Frank says.

I know what you are. Do you know who you are? She laughs. She used to sleep in my bed at night, the woman says. Falling asleep I would whisper *you and me* over and over. You and me. Yumi. Did she tell you that? I guess not, but that's what she heard. That's what she named herself. *She's* the friendly, you see? I'm as real as it gets, honey. She smiles.

Frank eyes her sympathetically. Is she that clueless about what she is? The longer friendlies exist, the more unstable they become. In moments like this he wonders if it would be so bad if the imaginary things overwhelmed the world? Sure, there would be nothing to distinguish what is real from what is fake, but what's so special about real things? Chernobyl was real. Velekete Market was real. The holes in his daughter's heart were real. Septal defect. It sounded like an imaginary disease. By the time they realized it was real, all he and his wife could do was sit idly by her bed singing songs to distract her as her heart kept beating and beating and the hole swallowed it.

The woman in the tub slurps up noodles which leave a sticky film on her teeth. She offers them to Frank who shakes his head. He'd rather drink a vial of the shit in the syringes he carries. The Jinx. Scientists invented it. The best the scientists could say was the friendlies were a kind of dark matter, absences in the emptiness of space that somehow corporealized, but with a little serum they could be Jinxed back into that nonexistence, departicalized back into dark matter. It made no sense whatsoever, but Frank joined the Sweepers anyway. Zeroing the zeroes, as the enlistment campaign encouraged. A few drops will make you numb, make your head spin for hours, but large doses are fatal. Frank doesn't touch the stuff anymore.

You're sweet on her, aren't you? the woman smiles, her voice quailing. She taps her fake purple fingernails on the porcelain, another finger twirling a lock of hair. If Frank didn't know better, he would have believed the two women were sisters, black and white, like keys on a piano. Funny, he thinks, how imaginary things are little echoes of ourselves.

That's not what I came for, Frank starts to explain, because he always likes to say something to the friendlies before finishing what he came for, but lately the words elude him. What do you say to nonexistent things before you make them nonexistent?

Look at me, the woman says. Her eyes are steady, piercing. Look at me and tell me, what did you come for?

Frank doesn't answer. Maybe Veronica was right. Maybe this is a kind of killing. Maybe he should just walk away, just pretend this never happened. The world is big enough for real things and figments of imagination and all different kinds of zeroes.

The woman explains she tried to get rid of Yumi. Wish her out of existence. Even prayed once. But she just wouldn't go away. Whenever she looked in the mirror Yumi was there. Even when she concentrated enough to get her to disappear for a few hours she felt her there, like a ghost.

Nobody tells you that about a friendly, the woman says dreamily. How they'll sail a burning boat down the river of your thoughts.

What's your name? Frank asks.

The woman in the tub smirks. Does it even matter? That's not what you came for. Your mind is made up. She laughs and Frank wonders if she's laughing to keep from crying.

Frank wishes Veronica were here. She would know what to say. Sometimes there are no words. One of his first solo runs was to this little apartment shared by a mother and her adult son. When he got there the pair was squabbling in the kitchen over the stew, so Frank started going room to room but couldn't find anything until he went into the boiler room and there was the decomposing corpse of the mother whose face had been smashed in. When it was over, the son stood in the kitchen while the Sweepers cleaned the hissing white stain the imaginary mother left on the linoleum. He had this look on his face like there were all these things he forgot to say when she was alive, and then brought her back and still never managed to say them.

I believe you, Frank says to the woman in the tub. He reaches out, touches the woman's arm gently. He's not sure why he says this, much less why he's touching her. But there's something about lies, that oldest species of the imaginary, that just sounds better than the real.

I believe you, he says again, as the needle disappears into her neck, but Frank tries not to believe what is happening.

He believes there is a God who will punish them for all their imagination. He believes when this is over, he will slump against the tub, breathless, trying to convince himself he doesn't know what he just did and the woman in white who has been standing in the doorway the whole time, watching with glee, will ask as her mouth crinkles, Why isn't she zeroing out? He believes he will walk through the door of his apartment later and without wanting and without trying, will find her waiting for him in the tent, the same size after all these years, her laughter the same as yesterday and the yesterday before that, like she's never been gone, spawned from the tangled vines in his mind. He believes they will play hide-and-go-seek and count the stars. He believes they will both say *rabbit* at the same time and she will shout *jinx!* He believes she will ask what are these white stains on the carpet, the walls, the ceiling? He believes he will comb her hair and ask what it feels like to be a zero and she will smile and laugh and say *daddy, don't be silly,* but of course he must believe this is all nonsense, just *colorless green ideas sleeping furiously*, and what is unbelievable is how zeroing something else makes him feel so real. What is unbelievable is how every night when the room gets quiet, when he curls up on the floor next to her fresh white stain, curled as if praying, he brings them back without wanting, the zeroes and the not zeroes, all of them, even the one right here with the purple fingernails combing his hair, her laughter like a judgment hanging over him, her hot breath whispering in his ear: You and me, baby, yes, you and me forever.

Susannah, Who

Susannah, who talks in her sleep.

Susannah, who likes cracking walnuts with bare hands.

Susannah, who still remembers her lines from *Annie Get Your Gun* in high school.

Susannah, who fills the gas canister at sunrise, dizzied by the fumes, barefoot as she stares at the audition flyer. Susannah, lost in a daydream, who spills gas on the asphalt and tries to soak it up with the hem of her dress. Hurrying back into the car as the old man taps on the window and asks, "You alright, miss?" Fine, fine, she nods, ignoring when he leans through the window and his face twists with disgust and mumbles, "What in God's name is that?"

Susannah, who had forgotten about the thing on the seat next to her like a gnarled catcher's mitt, soft and wet with sickly patches along the meaty edges, smiling warmly as she fumbles the keys and says, "It's just a stomach."

Susannah, who had watched as the woman in the diner said, "Here, it's yours," and reached down her throat. It came out like a slow, wet hiccup. "I won't be needing it any longer," the woman said.

Susannah, who scrubbed toilets, mopped floors, talked suicides out of suicide, bussed tables, cooked eggs over easy, offered marital advice. Susannah, who recently got a raise to $2.35 an hour, not counting tips.

Susannah, who held out her hands and said *thank you* as the stomach dripped juices between her fingers, the esophagus dangling like old jump rope. Because she wanted to scream. Because what else could she say at this hour when the diner was full of truckers sipping coffee and blue hairs poking eggs, and that kid playing peekaboo with his reflection in the window, because thank God it was just a stomach, because how many times had these graybeard perverts grabbed her ass and pretended that was a tip?

Susannah, who wore the same underwear three days in a row.

Susannah, who bought a bus ticket to Hollywood once a month and never used it. Susannah, who found the stomach where she forgot it on the diner kitchen cutting board, scored across the top like the cooks had been playing a game of tic-tac-toe.

Susannah, who called her father while waiting for the bus after her shift and listened to him complain about his hemorrhoids and the chemtrails and the nurses trying to poison him. "What did you do today, sweetie?"

Susannah, who stared at the stomach in the Styrofoam box in her fridge next to the jar of olives and told her father, "Nothing."

Susannah, who coming home from the audition talked with the neighbor in the stairwell, a foreign prostitute who wanted Susannah to translate a new love letter from one of her Johns. "I'll pay you back," the prostitute promised.

Susannah, who put the stomach on the table and traced a finger along the veins, thick, just the way she likes them. She could tell the blackened stomach lesions were cancerous, likely from uranium exposure, but thought the stomach smelled elegant, almost like her father, telling herself if more men smelled like this she might go home with them, confused why nobody had turned it into a cologne.

Susannah, who inserted a finger inside the stomach, hypnotized by the gentle sucking, the warm sensation of bile, then frightened when it wouldn't let go and quickly left it in the fridge for a week.

Susannah, who drove forty miles to visit her father at the nursing home. "You should eat more," he said, handing her a pudding cup. He saved them in the sock drawer for her visits. "Remember the night your mother left and all there was in the cupboard was pudding?" He reminded her of how they shared a spoon. "That's how I knew we would be okay," he said.

Susannah, who back in her apartment vomited the pudding on the kitchen floor. The stomach crawled from its hiding place behind the curtain and slurped it quietly.

Susannah, who later that night asked the stomach, "Would you like to watch a movie?"

Susannah, who only watched horror movies. The classics, like *Nosferatu* and *The Golem and the Dancing Girl*. But also obscure horror. Like *The Black Pit of Dr. M.* and *Vampyr*. And her favorite, the silent films of Ebba Lindkvist. They were so strange and beautiful. An Ebba Lindkvist film could be hallucinatory, like in *Born Stillborn* about a woman who resurrects her stillborn baby to torment the lover who abandoned her. Or melancholic, like in *The Swallows* about a scorned woman cooking a soup made with her menstrual blood to seduce an ex-lover. *This Little Piggy*, about a pig that eludes the slaughterhouse only to be a victim of strange experiments at the asylum before escaping to terrorize the local village, was devilishly funny.

Susannah, who didn't care about the characters or what happened. "I just like to hear the screams," she told the stomach.

Susannah, who bottled her screams in jars, arranging them on shelves in the closet.

Susannah, who held the stomach on her lap during the movie and felt safe. Like that moment after a man's finished and no longer trying to worm his way inside you, that brief moment when he becomes quiet and soft and vaguely human.

Susannah, who pried open one of the stomach sphincters and asked, "Can I scream inside you?"

Susannah, who came home from the graveyard shift at the diner and found the stomach on the windowsill, a stray cat nibbling the shriveled edge. She ate half the ramen noodles and fed the rest to the stomach, then listened as it digested, dribbling out a milky gruel from one end.

Susannah, who asked the stomach, "Do you think I could be in the movies?"

Susannah, who woke up and discovered the stomach on the floor in a pool of juices, like a deflated balloon. Who wondered if it was sick and took it to the park thinking it could use some fresh air. Who put it in the sandbox. Who called her boss and said she didn't think she could work her shift tonight. "It's an emergency," she said, but he told her not to bother coming back, told her she was a lousy waitress because she didn't share tips and ate all the leftovers.

Susannah, who searched the classifieds but didn't want to be a receptionist, or a hotel maid, or a kindergarten teacher. Who called her father who said he could get her a job at the nursing home cleaning bed pans. "I wiped your ass for years, now you can wipe mine," he laughed.

Susannah, who called her father an asshole as she hurried to the sandbox because the crows were trying to fly away with the stomach. "Jesus. What happened to your fucking dog?" one of the mothers said.

Susannah, who suddenly felt a tremendous affection for the stomach, almost like it was her child, and tied the esophageal tube in a knot at one end, creating a strap so she could carry the stomach on her shoulder and even smiled on the bus when a stranger asked, "Where did you get that amazing purse?"

Susannah, who lied and said it was a prop in a movie she filmed in Prague, feeling a vicious pleasure when the stranger looked at her own cheap purse with such disappointment.

Susannah, who clenched the stomach tighter to her chest as the bus rattled over potholes through the neighborhood. A man on the bus said, "You're the girl from the diner who brings me my oatmeal every Thursday."

Susannah, who looked at her feet, chewed her lip. "Oh, no, that's the other Susannah. I just work the graveyard shift."

Susannah, who tried to calm her father on the phone. "Don't drink the water," he cried, "how do you think I ended up in this place?"

Susannah, who hurried through the rain with the stomach under her shirt, pressed against her bare chest, then up the stairs where she collapsed on the rug, still clutching the stomach close to her, afraid of what might happen if she moved. "Don't worry," she told the stomach, "I'll be right here."

Susannah, who ate five packages of ramen and then checked the scale before looking at herself in the mirror, pinching the fat around her hips. "I know," she told the stomach, "bigger girls have better screams, and there's no Hollywood without screams."

Susannah, who stops at every gas station along the road to fill a new canister.

Susannah, who rolls down the window, choking on the fumes.

Susannah, who picked up four shifts at the nursing home. She bathed residents, emptied bed pans, changed catheters, picked lice, wiped asses, helped with arts and craft, mopped vomit, refilled pudding cups. After covering her father's expenses, she made $5.65 an hour.

Susannah, who looked out the window while her father was talking. "You're going to be famous. First this part, then the next. But first you need to lose a little weight. Then you'll have enough money to buy back the house and we can go home. Just the two of us."

Susannah, who told the bloated stomach after it finished the crackers and noodles and everything else in the cupboard, "Do you ever feel like murdering something?"

Susannah, who stared at the stomach and the stomach stared back.

Susannah, who laughed.

Susannah, who went dumpster diving but could not satisfy the stomach's hunger. Susannah, who still liked to pick dahlias off the side of the road, her mother's favorite.

Susannah, who the more she looked, the more she understood a stomach is a self-contained universe.

Susannah, who listened to the neighbor upstairs, then finished translating the letter. Susannah, who put another jar on the closet shelf.

Susannah, who traced a finger over the stomach and said, "You don't understand. You're just a stomach. No eyes, no ears, no throat. That's where your voice lives. Do you know voice? That thing that wants to sky wild like a balloon?"

Susannah, who threw the stomach in the trash, then repented.

Susannah, who stood in the rain outside the diner remembering when the blue hairs and graybeards used to say she looked like a movie star. "Don't forget us when you're famous," they used to say.

Susannah, who looked at her feet and chewed her lip when her father said, "You're too thin. No man will want a woman with hips like that." Susannah, who watched her father fill a glass under the tap and say, "There's nothing wrong with a little uranium in the water. If you drink enough, you see angels."

Susannah, who hates that fathers have the luxury of always contradicting themselves.

Susannah, who decided to perform the silent scream at her next audition. Like Lil Dagover when the somnambulist creeps into her room in *The Cabinet of Dr. Caligari*.

Susannah, who practiced all day in the bathroom. "How did that sound?" she asked the stomach.

Susannah, who after feeding the stomach the last of the ramen scrounged the gutter and alley, handing the cashier a dozen new packages of ramen as she counted out nickels and dimes.

Susannah, who cautiously put the bloated stomach in her mouth. Teeth gnawing rubbery edges. The stomach squirming, tasting like cheap cologne and coffee and pitchblende. She tried to swallow, but her tongue kept thrusting. The stomach hissed. There was a scream, but she wasn't sure if that was her or the stomach. "I'm sorry," she kept saying, rocking the trembling stomach back and forth. "I'm sorry."

Susannah, who took a handful of pills and woke up unable to remember why. She felt so refreshed, so alive, like Sleeping Beauty.

Susannah, who was still a little unsure. "Am I dead?" she asked the prostitute's lover on the stairwell. He took one look at Susannah with her stomach purse and scuttled away like a crab.

Susannah, who stared at the empty cupboards and listened to the stomach growling at her feet, then turned off the light and gave the stomach a bath in murky yellow water until patches of cancerous flesh glowed. She swirled her finger round and round the tub, licked it dry.

Susannah, who watched her father cough up blood into a kerchief, waiting to see what else might come up.

Susannah, who told her father to make up his goddamned mind. One day the water is poison, the next it's a cure-all. "Which is it?" she screamed. The old man wept.

Susannah, who knew her father was not her real father. "I found you at a park all alone," he often said, "abandoned by your parents." He waved his arms as the nurses came to sedate him. "And this is how you repay me?"

Susannah, who went to the library and looked up the Greek word *pharmakon*. It means both poison and remedy. No relation to *pharmakos*, which meant ritualistic sacrifice, or scapegoat.

Susannah, whose head ached from too many words.

Susannah, who walked into the high school gymnasium full of other girls and went straight to the table where a pudgy man with glasses shuffled through papers. "I'm here for the audition," she said. She removed the flyer from her pocket and smoothed out the wrinkles. The man took her headshot and gave her a number.

Susannah, who looked around the room at all the pretty girls, clenching the stomach purse closer to her and asked, "What kind of Hollywood movie is it?"

Susannah, who felt something in the pit of her own stomach when he said, "It's just a hemorrhoid commercial."

Susannah, who went through the closet after the break-in and found all the jars shattered, and in the fridge the olives missing. But the stomach was still there, tied to the bedpost. "Have you noticed anything unusual?" the police officer said.

Susannah, who rolled over in the middle of the night and whispered to the stomach on the pillow, "Remember the scream I left inside you? Can I listen to it? I have no idea what I sound like."

Susannah, who stood naked in the mirror and felt the bones under her skin and knew she was not a universe, just an odd basket of atoms.

Susannah, who pours gasoline over the steps, the porch, the door. Crawls through a broken window and splashes gasoline over the carpet, the furniture, the walls.

Susannah, who comes to the top of the stairs and feels lost even though she never forgot this place, her childhood house, with its creaking floors, its dripping pipes, the way sunlight trickled through windows.

Susannah, who remembers the laughter, the crying, the slammed doors. She listens to the echo in her ear. Not like a bell or a buzz, but a faraway voice. The air is a perfume of dahlias. She takes a deep breath and follows it down the hall.

Susannah, who finds a stranger wheezing in bed. The window is open. It's freezing. "You came," the old woman says, trying to sit up. She waves a hand gently, beckoning Susannah to come closer. "They said you wouldn't come. But I knew, I just knew."

Susannah, who's never seen the stranger before, who's unsure if she's a hallucination or really there, walks cautiously into the room. The old woman's hair is silver, her body beneath the gown yellow and thin. Her feet hang off the bed. "You're sick," Susannah says, sitting on the edge of the mattress. "We're all a little sick these days, my darling," the old woman smiles, "but that doesn't matter now. You're here." She pulls fingers through Susannah's hair, tells her how pretty she is. When she shivers, Susannah can't resist the urge to hold her hand. "You came home," the old woman says over and over.

Susannah, who can't bring herself to ruin the old woman's delusions, who pretends to be the daughter she's not.

Susannah, who with some hesitation takes the stomach and slices it down the middle with the letter opener from the nightstand, butterflies it with both hands, pulling at the fibrous tissue until the stomach spreads over the old woman like a blanket. She stops shivering. Her breaths slow. "Cigarette," the old woman says, her voice raspy.

Susannah, who reaches into the drawer and the room fills with smoke.

Susannah, who apologizes for disturbing the old woman and stands to leave. "Stay awhile, please," the old woman says, the stomach wrapping around her tighter, the juices gurgling, the flesh syncing its pulses to the rhythm of the old woman's sweaty breaths.

Susannah, who tells the old woman she's an actress.

Susannah, who keeps the old woman company by pantomiming the part of the forest nymph in the Ebba Lindkvist film *Skogsrå*: seducing the lumberjack cutting down her forest and turning him into a tree during the great famine when starving peasants made bread out of bark.

Susannah, who holds the old woman's hand, smiles, and they smoke more cigarettes.

Rewilding

It's my fourth time this week at the clinic waiting for my rewilding. The pamphlet says I could come back a penguin. Or an elephant. Or a frog. I'm not picky. But it would be nice to wake up one of those King Kong monkeys that roamed the jungles before the last Ice Age. Six months ago, they tried to put cousin Margaret on chemo for the third time but she ripped out the tubes and marched herself to a clinic. Now she's a panda. All the bamboo she can eat and nobody wiping her ass. The preserve sends a picture every month.

My husband is across the street on a tour of the Mormon temple, probably still wearing his headset listening to the disembodied voice like gravel in a bucket.

Press one for WHO ARE YOU? (God's child).
Press two for WHERE DID YOU COME FROM? (outer space).
Press three for WHERE ARE YOU GOING? (maybe heaven, but the odds are slim).

A few minutes ago, the disembodied voice was pointing out the sign FAMILIES CAN BE FOREVER while I wrangled my kids licking Cheetos off the floor as my husband whispered in my ear about the baby in heaven waiting to be incubated and I imagined him on top of me as I stared out the hotel window at the smirking golden angel statue who can't decide if he should blow the goddamn trumpet or hurl himself from the spire.

The nurse hands me a stack of forms. Answering honestly will expedite my chances of a suitable conversion, she smiles.

Is it ever safe for the chicken to cross the road?

How do you feel about God's policies towards animals?

If a male barber shaves all and only those men who do not shave themselves, does he shave himself?

Why do dogs understand human words, but we can't understand barking?

Are plants farming us, supplying oxygen until we die and become compost they can digest? Show your math.

Is cereal soup?

Under ALLERGENS I put cartwheels, having never actually done one in all my life.

The clinic is beneath an abandoned factory. Just to get to the door you have to walk down several flights of stairs and show everyone your teeth. It's all very hush-hush. Rewilding is still a novelty, and the conversion rate is frighteningly low. But since the extinctions, living in a city is its own kind of Russian roulette. Better to take three pharmaceutical cocktails and wake up on a wildlife preserve without a care in the world. If you agree to the terms of service, your name is inscribed on the wall and your family gets to choose between a snow cone machine and an electric toothbrush. I hope they choose the toothbrush.

Most of the volunteers with me have seen better days. Blue hairs and addicts and army vets missing limbs. I'm young, I'm healthy, and I'm fertile. The pamphlet says I'm an ideal candidate.

My husband says rewilding is bullshit, a bunch of pussies running away from the problem, but in the same breath he talks about coming back as an orca. Eat everyone, he says. I'd be happy as something soft. Like an octopus. Masters of camouflage with nine brains and three hearts. They probably do cartwheels all day.

The woman sitting next to me fills out her questionnaire. She fidgets, fussing with her hair which smells like ammonia, no doubt distressed at the thought of rewilding as a beetle or anchovy. Under ALLERGENS I can't help but notice she has an extensive history.

Plums: Moderate. Broken clavicle falling out of tree trying to sneak out of foster home.

Dogs: Severe. Dentist extracted supernumerary canine tooth. Only childhood friend a spider unable to spin webs that ate sugar granules from fingertips.

Wool: Mild. Tied up with scarf during drama club rehearsal of Antigone.

Eggs: Moderate. Anaphylaxis from gin fizz at anthropology soiree. Ovaries equally inhospitable.

Ragweed: Severe. Walked the 37th parallel hoping to be abducted by extraterrestrials. It was a mistake, I believe, having been born human.

It's easy to fall in love with strangers. But she has the face of an ibex, pretty in an awkward way, and I have the clumsy hands of a lobster, so I know we'll never be goldfish in some pond doomed to fall in love over and over when our memories lapse every seven seconds. Still, when the allergic woman goes to submit her paperwork, I stumble into her. I don't know why I act this way. I don't open my door to happiness. When she knocks it means her cousin catastrophe is creeping through your window. We exchange shy smiles and apologies as my fingertips glance hers.

They lead all the volunteers down another flight of stairs and through a maze of tunnels with flickering lights. Doyennes in messy surgical scrubs flank us on either side. Janitors scrub greasy streaks off the floor.

I know I'm going to run before getting to the end of the hall, run up the stairs and back to a minivan with a kind but stupid husband and six vultures under six, but for a moment I imagine walking into the rewilding chamber. There will be soft music. We'll drink the cocktails, nervously at first, then licking the glass rims with gusto. They'll bathe and perfume us. As they strap us into the gurneys, the allergic woman will tell me she has a tattoo nobody has ever seen. There's a faraway sadness on her face as she wonders if after she rewilds will it be a birthmark, a scar, or just disappear?

My head gets cloudy. I can see the tattoo on her hip. Five little black geometries in a line. Play. Pause. Stop. Rewind. Fast-forward. Only I'm not sure which skin button to push.

Will she know I'm imagining us grazing the icy steppe, two little no-nonsense ibex bitches bleating pleasantries, escaping snow leopards as we leap cliff to cliff, the caprine equivalent of cartwheels?

What do you think they made in this factory? she'll ask dreamily.

And then I'll open my hand into hers, already the fingers gnarling into something else.

Paperclips, maybe?

Teeth Like God's Shoeshine

We're in the boiler room playing the Mormon underwear game. Honey sits across from me in the rusty tub that cradles us like a lullaby. The light bulb flickers and hums. One. Two. Three. Once Honey has the underwear on, Lulu hands me the knife we found in the neighbor's closet. Crooked, but it can slice through a tomato easy peasy. Honey fidgets nervously with his fingers until the knuckles are ghost white. I tell him it's just a game, but it's so much more than that.

Lulu explains the rules. First you put on the underwear. Then you say the name. Then the knife. The name is the most important. Say it slow, I always tell the newbies like Honey, or the game is over before it begins. Every night it's a new name. Like a speakeasy. Say the name and the curtain opens and you get to see how far the yellow brick road really goes.

And then what, I'm a Mormon? Honey laughs. He's got fancy white teeth like God's shoeshine. The Mormon underwear droops off him like a second skin. We stole it from a clothesline an hour ago. The Mormons always leave them out to dry on Sundays, flapping in the breeze like alien pajamas. Honey looks like a doofus, but his hair is still dreamy.

I just always want to lick him, Lulu whispers in my ear.

Lulu was born upstairs but says she doesn't live here anymore. The windows are all punched out and the doors are slipping off hinges. She's been playing the game forever, since before the sun burned a hole through the sky and the water disappeared. Lulu's one of those girls with a clever tongue. She whistles, gleeks, twists it to look like a cloverleaf. Licks things to feel their pain. Lately, she clicks her tongue to speak with animals. Mice, wasps, crickets. If it weren't for her tongue, I don't know what we'd do.

Try not to flinch, I remind Honey, steadying the knife.

You sure this won't hurt? Honey says, his face suddenly dumb as a rabbit. Honey's parents are dead. Killed by nefarious Mormons over a century-old fry sauce recipe. Oh, Honey, I want to say, this will hurt. Don't you know magic?

We teach him. Once, a woman and her friend were gossiping in the kitchen when a gas line exploded, frying them top to bottom like tomatoes, but the Mormon woman was wearing her underwear so all she got was a bad sunburn. Once, a Kennecott miner was sprayed with acid mist that ate through his clothes and blistered and peeled his skin raw except where he was covered with Mormon underwear. Once a rapist had his dick burned off when it got too close to the Mormon underwear.

There's no magic without pain, I tell all the newbies, and no belief without magic. It comes rushing through you like a waterfall. Why else play the game?

Honey is no different. One minute he's sitting there saying, Who are you talking to? Are we gonna play or what? and then I put the knife in him. He squirms like a porpoise on roller skates, but I hold him close until he becomes my second skin.

It's hard to explain the feeling of a second skin. Sometimes it's like a big curtain smothering you, and other times it's like your body's been hammocked between trees and some stranger crawls inside to master your great secret. Then the room gets warm and I can see traces of all the Mormons who used to live in this house, summoned when we say their names. The dead like to watch the game, I guess, remembering all the magic they left behind. That's all they have left.

I wait for Honey to figure out if he's staying or going. Sometimes the curtain opens fast and other times it opens slow. It's different for everyone. His eyes roll back until they are two white marbles. The red scaly crusts around his sockets are like sci-fi weirdo glasses. Boys like him walk in circles around what's left of the old Salt Lake collecting brine flies in jars. They sell them to the beauty salons where rich ladies pay to have the flies eat the flaky rash off their skins so they look like porcelain figurines in a museum.

Now can I lick him? Lulu whispers, her voice so far away and the shape of her so dim I could hardly see her. Heat buzzes through the window, tickling my ear.

I tell the newbies to keep their eyes open during the game, but the truth is I always close my eyes. I put the knife in and close my eyes and time flips sideways like a turtle on its shell. Time is a game too. The hands of a clock are like chutes and ladders: sometimes you slide down and sometimes you climb up and sometimes the gears go wonky and you just spin. I've seen so many things in time. I see my wrinkled body floating in the lake like a gherkin, and blowing out birthday candles, and the way my skin goosebumps listening to coyote howls in the canyon. I see all the things that have been, and will be, and might have been like twisted slivers in a kaleidoscope.

But not with Honey. With Honey I leave my eyes open. I want to see nothing.

I wonder how other people go through life like this.

Wife No. 57

Devotees of Brigham Young will not be surprised to learn that before the Mormon prophet died just after four o'clock in the afternoon, he propped himself on imported silk pillows and amid the careless aroma of burnt juniper whispered his last feverish words. Orson Pratt, the eccentric mathematician and official Church historian at the time, recorded the dying seer exclaiming *Joseph! Joseph! Joseph!* in anticipation of being reunited with his beloved martyred friend. The evening edition of the *Tribune*, however, claimed the American Moses sighed *I loved them all,* ostensibly referring to his well-documented paramours. But my great-great-grandfather, Phineas Gustaf Habermeyer, a dentist recently emigrated from Bavaria who had the enviable task of making the death mask, said the prophet quietly summoned his maidservant and in a series of inaudible but zealous whispers made her promise once he died she would bathe and perfume him and as a final gesture of goodwill "stick [her] fingers up [his] arse spigot and twirl counter-clockwise" so he might meet the Lord with both spirit and flesh clean. The official certificate confirms peritonitis as the cause of death. Scribbled across the top in my ancestor's inscrutable penmanship are the words, *The Lion of the Lord now roars into the eternities.* An obvious lie, but ecclesiastical hyperbole is unavoidable.

No sooner had the prophet died than my ancestor set to work. He applied plaster bandages to the greased face. He was more anxious about the molding cracking than nature reclaiming the prophet's body which soon began to bloat in the August heat. Removing the plaster hours later, my ancestor set about the more difficult task of fashioning an impression of the prophet's tongue. This unusual request, confirmed by various historians, came from the dying seer himself who wished the saints might one day visit a museum of all things Mormon and see a replica of his tongue, the "mighty mouthpiece of the Lord and…only thing this [desert?] feared in its hundred-million-year existence." Circling the deathbed, the elders watched curiously as my ancestor mixed beeswax and turpentine with gutta-percha soaked in boiling water to create a thermoplastic polymer, a chemical process that wouldn't be perfected for more than half a century. Now nearly dawn, he wedged open the prophet's mouth but found no tongue. Just a jagged, fleshy stump—forked and spackled with a necropolis of black ulcers. Phineas, who'd been with the body all night, swore it made a noise, "a kind of laugh," he later told his wife. Along with the other confused elders he turned to the maidservant for explanation, but she was gone.

They called her Sally. Her name might have been Kahpeputz, but after she was purchased in 1847 the prophet couldn't pronounce her indigenous name, so he called her Sally. He had no choice but to own her, he would later confess. The slave trader, a Ute shaman who went by the name Baptiste traveling up and down the valley selling native and Mexican children, had already slit the throat of a young boy—her brother, perhaps—and promised to do the same to the girl if nobody purchased her. It's possible the dumbfounded pilgrims stood at the auction block waiting, like Abraham, for an angel to intervene. Finally, one of the prophet's wives reluctantly offered a rifle in exchange for the small, thin girl whose body was a labyrinth of knife scars and festering burns, her skin smeared in blood and ashes.

It was out of love, the prophet insisted, that they bought her. Sally must have heard this excuse frequently. Bedridden for his final months, the prophet relied on his adopted daughter and Paiute servant to feed him, bathe him, transcribe his sermons, and his favorite: oil his little lion's beard until it glistened. His children no longer visited. His wives assumed he was already dead. So, Sally listened to the old raconteur confess. Maybe she requested this story. Not out of pity or to help him make penance, but for the pleasure of hearing her life was indistinguishable from a weapon.

Around the same time the elders discovered the missing tongue, Sally was likely in a stagecoach disappearing into the western dustbowl. I picture her gasping awake, her hands instinctively grasping her throat in search of the necklace. For a moment her body might have stiffened as she worried the noise wrestling her from her dream was the necklace swept away by the wind, then relieved it was only the driver shooting at pheasants. Against her chest the necklace prickled her damp skin.

Picture her raising the shade, squinting. The desert is a pale naked thing. Suddenly, the old words came back to her. *Tav'-o-kun.* The name her people gave this country. Place of the sun. My colleague suggested she would have traveled by night as much as possible to avoid the oppressive heat, but the stagecoach receipt stamped at 6:37 AM on 30 August containing the expected creases and yellowing is indisputable. It is the only record of Sally's signature. Thick, bold cursive strokes, undeniably elegant. The driver's name is illegible, the victim of an ink blot.

She could have taken the train. Transit authority records indicate the night cabin left the Salt Lake station for Lucin at 11:14. Was she afraid of the night? The furious silence of stars, their wild melancholy? Or was traveling by stage-coach, as one newspaper pundit expressed, a seductive misery reserved for the poor and faithful? Maybe she assumed the elders would expect her on the train. As a woman caught between three worlds, Sally must have known confused men do strange things. She likely told herself once she got to the salt flats she'd be safe. She could not yet imagine how upon her return she'll be married off to a Ute chief, nor how by the end of the year his jealous first wife will slit her throat and sprinkle a ring of salt around her shallow grave. The more wicked the soul, the belief goes, the more salt is needed to keep it from escaping the afterlife.

———

A few hours into the journey, the stagecoach would have stopped to water the horses. The driver— McCarthy, as best as I can decipher—skinned the pheasants and roasted them. Months later he will admit to escorting Sally to the salt flats but will not recall what she did nor the exact location. She bewitched me, he will supposedly inform the elders, which probably saved him from losing his wives, or worse, excommunication (although I can't find reliable sources to corroborate either of these claims).

They ate in silence. They followed the dust.

Half-asleep, Sally might have imagined the elders shuffling around the room as the little lion was fashionably embalmed and prepared for burial, their faces confused—except for my ancestor off in the corner humming as he penned a funeral hymn. *Farewell, dear brother, Brigham Young / God called thee through th' eternal gate, / Thy fame shall dwell on every tongue / And Saints thy worth will emulate.* The old men with sun-kissed faces nodding their heads and murmuring in agreement.

North of Tooele, a couple joined Sally in the carriage: a man with an oily moustache and a woman with her neck wrapped in pearls. A few pleasantries were likely exchanged and it's plausible the couple mentioned the drought and wondered why the prophet had not yet called down rain from the heavens. Probably because the little lion of the lord was called back to the zoo, Sally might have thought. Swallowing a laugh, we can imagine her clutching her chest to feel the necklace again. The couple would have been uncomfortable with her there, a so-called savage woman dressed in their clothes, unaware that Sally would have been nervous to look these strangers in the eye, which is why she removed a book from a fold in her dress and thumbed the pages. She might have remembered when the author, an Englishman, visited the Beehive House and gifted it to her. Having exhausted himself in the far East, he'd traveled West hoping to write an exotic tale of the prophetic American sultan and his desert harem. The pages were yellowed from her fingertips. Why hadn't they taught her to read like the other servants? Why did she have to study the scribbles by candlelight, teaching herself word after word, training her tongue like the woman in the story, Scheherazade, who knew that in any desert the tongue is the only way to keep your head from spinning? The book and the necklace were all Sally had now. How often the little lion told her that even if she married him, there would be no inheritance for her in this life or the next. "What God has cursed even I cannot undo," he told her. And yet, on the 1870 U.S. Census she is listed as *Wife No. 57*.

The book, somewhat miraculously, has survived in the Utah State Historical Society collections. The text is in pristine but unremarkable condition, except for a single dog-eared page, the tale of Tawaddud on the 437th night, which Sally must have been reading as the stagecoach churned west. Perhaps the pearl-throated woman asked if Sally liked tales of the East? Unaccustomed to being acknowledged, Sally would have closed the book, smiled, and pretended not to understand English.

When the little lion preached on Sundays, Sally couldn't quite understand the words so she watched his mouth. Among her people—day after day a blur in her memory—leaders were supposed to have a way with words too. She couldn't understand when the little lion said, *We are the salt of the earth, brethren, and must flavor her whether she wants it or not*, but the way his mouth moved between smile and grimace and solemnity was wildly enchanting. The sound of him was enough to want to follow him anywhere.

As reported in the now infamous *New York Times* interview, the prophet's hygiene was exceptional. He owned many things. Trinkets, books, maps, wives. The whole valley essentially. But he treated his tongue as his prized possession. At night, Sally brought him an assortment of tonics on a silver tray. She watched as he removed his gold-plated dentures before rinsing and gargling and spitting into a porcelain basin. With a bristled comb, he removed a thin white film off his tongue. Sometimes he would ask her about her day, other times talk about the weather, almost always proposing marriage. She refused. But with a smile. Even if the lion is little, we can imagine her thinking, one must always smile.

It's no surprise that Sally was the first to notice the spots on his gums. White patches, slowly darkening. They spread over his tongue like constellations. His mouth tingled at first, then ached, then burned. Soon it became difficult for the prophet to talk. My ancestor had no idea how to treat the infection, but from secondhand letters we learn Sally proposed a remedy. Wandering deep into the canyons, far away from the hissing trains, she returned with purple sage, penstemon, lizard tail, and sego lily. The last one scared the prophet. Several of his children had died from mistaking toxic camas for the medicinal sego lily. To his untrained eye they looked the same.

Coaxing the prophet's tongue out of his mouth, Sally must have pinched it like a slug between two fingers and gently massaged the lesions with the herbal paste. He gagged and whined, the tongue disappearing back into his mouth like a snake coiling in its grotto. Wrestling the tongue out again, she squeezed the flesh until the pustules burst. With surprising candor, the prophet's journals admit to fainting. She turned other herbs into a slurry he swished around his mouth and swallowed. It gave him diarrhea. We can only imagine what he was thinking, the so-called mouthpiece of the Lord, as he wrapped his arms around the neck of a so-called savage woman and clung to her like a baby chimp as she wiped his backside clean.

When I submitted the request slip for the "Plural Wives" artifacts at the Gardo House Historical Society in downtown Salt Lake City, the archivist looked annoyed. Upon returning, she informed me the bin in question was missing—an unusual but not abnormal development—and the necklace I was trying to locate was lost. As substitute, she provided a grainy photograph of Amelia Folsom Young, the twenty-fifth and favorite wife, to better visualize the gift from the little lion. I humored her, feeling more vindicated than disappointed.

The fact that Sally was wearing the silver necklace on her way to the salt flats is indisputable to all but the most passionate skeptics. The only distinguishing feature between the necklace in the photograph and the one Sally wore the night she unbuttoned her fussy collar somewhere between Wendover and Salt Lake City along what is now interstate-80 was the tongue fastened at one end like a monstrous pendant.

Cupped in Sally's palm, the tongue would have seemed like a fat baby lizard. *Tiki*, her people called them. The venomous Gila monster Sally knew not to chase as a girl. No doubt it had a pungent odor. Luckily, the stagecoach driver was asleep. Sally could tell by the way his breaths made the hairs of his beard dance. The men of her people had smooth faces, like stones polished in riverbeds, but the pale settlers loved looking like wild dogs.

Removing salt from a pouch she generously coated the tongue. She wasn't sure why she did this. She wanted to swim to the bottom of the ocean, to the Old Woman of the Sea who carved the first people and hide the tongue among the coral, far away from this place. But she wasn't sure if she believed in that magic anymore, or if the Old Woman would recognize her as one of her daughters. She put the necklace back on and buttoned the collar. All night she would feel it between her breasts, unsure if she was sweating or if the tongue was somehow salivating.

In reviewing the archives of the Utah Botanical Society, I remain unsure what herbs Sally used to treat what the prophet documented in letters as a "disturbing infection." Yarrow, milkweed, and bitterbrush are the likely suspects. Church historians have long rumored that the "savage woman" poisoned their beloved prophet, but the history of apologetics is riddled with confusions of conspiracy with divinity. By the time my ancestor was summoned, the cancer had metastasized. The tongue was now swollen and yellowed with silvery patches spidering inside his cheeks. Like all Habermeyer men, my ancestor was not fond of blood and likely discouraged amputation. But whether the prophet—who did like blood—saw no other choice, or if Sally seduced his imagination, there's no doubt it was Sally who anesthetized the prophet before severing the tongue at the root.

She must have been surprised at how long it was. *Like a worm*, scribbled in the margins of her copy of the *Arabian Nights*. Rinsing it off, she then submerged the tongue in a spirit of wine and turpentine. Before sealing the decanter, she added a handful of black pepper and a pinch of mustard seed. Perched on the prophet's desk, the tongue floated like a shipwrecked castaway, a macabre but enchanting conversation piece for any visitor.

From varied sources we know that months after the amputation, Sally entered the room carrying her usual tray of tonics and herbs and found the prophet armed with a scalpel and magnifying glass. Spread over the desk was the dissected tongue: a hundred pieces of muscle, nerves, veins, and papillae arranged in rows like miniature cobblestone streets. Did he smile with childish pride at this butchery? Or did he immediately try to pacify a disturbed Sally by dipping a spoon in a nearby jar of honey and drizzling it over a lump of tongue? She must have been confused as he smacked his lips and nodded enthusiastically. *Taste!* he scribbled on the little chalkboard hung around his neck.

She agreed to serve as his apprentice. Was there another choice? Sally pinching the half-rotted tongue between her fingers to see if the prophet groaned in unison. He did. Sally massaging salt, gravy, herbs, and ashes into the flesh and the blindfolded prophet identifying each substance in turn.

It lives that once was dead, he presumably wrote on the chalkboard.

Throughout the winter he was a ghost, locked away in his study dissecting the tongue, fingers blackened with ink, his constant notebook scribbling like matrimonial roaches. When Sally awoke to half-garbled screams one night, she found the little lion kneeling on the floor in a weeping rage trying to tear out the insides of his mouth. Insomnia had turned his beard white. She helped him into bed as he gestured to his mouth, murmuring. No amount of water quenched the burning in his throat. He convulsed for hours. Eventually, he fainted from the pain.

But the burning sensations only intensified. He sweated through four shirts a day. The only relief came from bathing the amputated tongue in laudanum which made him a grumpy narcoleptic.

When he handed her the pamphlet after the spring thaw, Sally was likely nervous. The prophet was pale and haggard with wild eyes like two glossy marbles. She read slowly. She knew he was prone to tantrums he liked to call revelation, but each page was worse than the one before. I attempted to access the extant copy of what historians have nicknamed *Discourses of My Cloven Tongue*, but the skylit reading room at the Utah State Historical Society was under renovation yet again. Momentarily defeated, I thumbed through my ancestor's medical ledger at the nearby Daughters of the Utah Pioneers Museum where I found the following much-cited passages scribbled in the margins as if in a daydream. The condensed "sermon of the queerest sort," to parse my ancestor, reasoned the Holy Spirit still lived within the prophet's amputated tongue. "For thus the evangelist promised, *The tongue is a fire*. And we know the Holy Spirit dwells in eternal burnings. Ergo, my tongue is the domicile of the Holy Spirit on this earth." Towards the end brother Brigham warned, "Mock me not, learned men. Why else would the psalmist say, *There is not a word in my tongue, but, lo, O Lord, thou placed it there?* That revelations from heaven even now burn anxiously on my cloven tongue is indisputable. But, bereft of the holy appendage as I am, through what mechanism might we provoke their release?"

The little lion did not lack in imagination. He baptized the tongue in consecrated oil, demanding it reveal its secrets, but this proved ineffective. Luckless and desperate, he purchased an Edison battery. Electricity was all the rage in 1877.

The telegraph sent messages halfway across the globe. Hysterical women cured with shock therapies. Soldiers juiced with currents in Crimea. "The soul is electric," traveling exhibitions declared. Even Edison said electricity "might yet prove the link between this world and the one beyond." Using an electrode coil, the prophet showered his tongue in a hiss of blue sparks. Other than making all the cats in the neighborhood yowl, this only succeeded in slightly cooking the tongue and provoking Sally's annoyance. *I speak with a cloven tongue of fire*, the prophet wrote defiantly on his chalkboard. Not anymore, Sally likely told him.

By late spring he was bedridden. The pain in his mouth migrated to his abdomen. As death proved inevitable, he said his only worry was he might have to wait "a long season of silence" to be reunited with his tongue. Four days before the end he was still busy revising the pamphlet the Church to this day claims is a hoax. "It is a wild thing," he scribbled beside a shaky illustration of his dissected tongue, "and regrettably I cannot tame it."

While the elders debated whether the pamphlet was a forgery, Sally trekked into the salt flats. It was 31 August. Stepping from the stagecoach she was almost blinded by the white, ghostly corpse of an ancient ocean.

She required a hatchet to carve open the salt-crusted earth. The constant flooding, freezing, thawing, and evaporating of water across the flats create hexagonal veins like salted honeycomb.

Removing the necklace, Sally might have admired how she had stitched the tongue back together so seamlessly that God himself could not distinguish whether it was her handiwork or his. She wedged it inside a small glass jar and filled it with handfuls of salt. I suppose it's possible, as one meddlesome colleague has suggested, that as she buried it she remembered the night before the amputation, how the little lion stared at his face in a small, mottled mirror. He'd made it when he was a glazier, in the life he had before conversion, before God called him. He did this nightly, always remembering how one afternoon he stood before a crowd and, for a few seconds, his face and voice seemed like his dead prophet-friend. The miracle of my life, he believed.

As several thousand mourners packed into the tabernacle for the funeral, Sally rode back into town and confessed to the elders she had no choice. The mourners sang my ancestor's hymn (*Farewell, dear brother, Brigham Young . . . Thy fame shall dwell on every tongue*), unaware the Lord's mouthpiece was a hundred miles away buried under two feet of salt. She confessed everything she did was out of love. She confessed there is not enough salt.

After the End of Color

The color librarian comes out at night because that is when it is easiest to collect the color. He moves slowly but deliberately past houses teeming with ivy, pinching a bit of violet from a crack in the sidewalk and fisting a handful of orange off a mailbox. The color is soft, grainy. Neither wet nor dry. It's early but his hands already ache. He pauses, removes his glasses to rub eyes that feel as though there is a smoldering match behind them.

It used to take a few minutes to fill the bucket, back when a menace of color blanketed the city, but now he is lucky to fill half the bucket on any given night.

Tonight, like all nights, he lifts the reds to his lips. He knows the color is tasteless and yet when he swallows reds he can taste them.

It is hard to say whether he is good at his job because not even the color librarian is sure what his job is. He tries not to think about it. He tries not to think about the broken windows or rusted bicycles or wonder why he wears a watch but never thinks about time. He tries not to think about the pointlessness of his days and the exhaustion of his nights or the paradox of light—how sometimes it bends and other times reflects, or how light always seems to know where it's going, always stretching, always searching for clean blank spaces. Most of all, he tries not to take his eyes off the road and glance up at the rainbow and its brittle band of light, sad that he will not live long enough to understand the language of color.

———————

The rainbow came on a Wednesday. A few children spent the afternoon pretending it was a stairwell to a lost kingdom and climbed trees trying to reach it. A week passed before anyone in the city realized it wasn't a normal rainbow, refusing to leave the skyline, stubbornly stretched in the same arc. By the end of the month crowds gathered frequently to watch it, perched like gulls, unblinking. Its colors seemed to intensify. The bands thickened, flickering gently at the edges.

It was a popular attraction. Families gathered at the park with picnic baskets and binoculars. There was music and dancing. Vendors sold brightly colored food. This upset the roller-skating rink and movie theatre owners because how could they compete with a rainbow? Florists saw their business triple. People wanted to believe in the rainbow. It could not just be light bending around moisture, could it? It must be something else, something more. A dream strained from a nightmare. For the skeptics a new physics, for the believers the hand of God. People in hot-air balloons and hang gliders tried to float through the rainbow. Others stared at it from below, curved in the sky like a hot blind scar.

———————

The color librarian pauses at Brigham Young's old Beehive House. Halfway up the porch steps he offers a rat a bite of cheese. Like most of the city, the Beehive House is smeared in grime, in moss, in mold. Just looking at it makes his bones ache and hands cramp. He used to come to a nearby park with his wife to catch fireflies. Before the blackouts, before the rationing, she would have a dozen jars full of them in the nursery. The color librarian always thought the fireflies were hideous, but he couldn't take his eyes off them. I like to think they're praying, his wife would say whenever their bodies flickered.

Less than a year after the rainbow's arrival it started shedding. Millions of flakes an hour, coating the city in a strange dust. A panel of scientists from the Observatory stood on the gymnasium stage and pointed to charts and spoke about radiational cooling in the lower troposphere bending light at a slower rate which makes rainbows defy the laws of classical mechanics.

What risk does the rainbow pose for children? people wanted to know. Nature does not take risks, the Observatory said. At what point is it not just a rainbow but a sign of something else? A rainbow is not a sign, it can only be a rainbow, the Observatory said. Other questions went unanswered. When will it do something? Can we weaponize it for world peace? Can we nominate it for mayor? What happens if someone touches the rainbow? Is there such a thing as refracted light infection?

It is a sign from God, someone said.

It's science, someone interrupted.

There is no exact science except for God, said another.

The color librarian is not sure if God put the rainbow in the sky or if science is coming unhinged. Before seeing the bodies stacked up in ditches, their insides turned outside, the color librarian believed God was a clockmaker with a sense of humor to build a machine like us, and even now he would like to imagine a patient God who leaves blank spaces in the canvas for humans to fill in, but after the bombs, the suicides, the evacuations, the sewers, now that he is alone with the quiet that is both beautiful and frightening, such belief leaves the color librarian with more questions than answers. He does not know if he is lucky, or immune, or being punished, or maybe he is a fairy godfather gathering up the dust of some botched spell.

Did you do it? his wife asked that evening, as if in a trance, Is it finished? He had stayed off the main road coming back from the lake, soaked to the waist, glancing over his shoulder. Already she was throwing its things into the fire: towels, pacifier, shoes, blankets. All infected, she said. Removing his wet clothes, she added them to the fire. It hissed. Not the pillow, he said, his hands still trembling and feeling as if he had drowned. Later, after she was gone, he would board up the windows and sit in the room with the empty crib until it was quiet.

It was no use telling her she didn't have to go. If you stay, you're dead, she said. If you go, he told her, it's just a different kind of dying.

She believed she'd seen the face of God in the sewers. The ark, they called it. He told her to wait up here a little longer. Things might change. Things have already changed, she said. Won't it make you sad to stay here with all this color? she asked from the doorway. Hugging the pillow to his chest he told her, I am always sad.

———————

He almost doesn't notice the body in the gutter. Matted fur, pink skin now a greenish black. It smells like old cheese. How did he not see it a week ago?

He brushes away maggots, swats at wasps trying to lay eggs. The patch of hardened yellow skin on the throat reminds the color librarian of the early days of the rainbow, when at recess children played Leprechaun, which was really just a violent game of hide-and-go-seek. Once he watched the hidden child being tackled, punched, kicked, slapped, and scratched until bruised. Then it was someone else's turn. Sweaty and exhausted, the child most bruised who wasn't crying won.

He leaves most animals where he finds them, gifting their bodies to the inevitabilities of time. But not the little ones. These he buries in the cemetery. The one place he hates going. The one place in the city he doesn't clean, the gravestones forever spackled with bright dead color.

———————

The color librarian carefully scoops dust off the steps. Later, he'll sort the color into jars in the library basement. Oranges, reds, blues. Color is strange. Most of the time it is dusty. Occasionally stringy. Sometimes like grains of sand. Each hue has its own personality. He is not sure what they will do with this library of color in the future. Maybe it will save them. Maybe it will tell them how to stop this from happening again. Maybe they will do nothing at all. Indifference is a pleasant disease, killing slowly and kindly. He likes to stare at the jars in the darkness of the library basement, the dust glowing faintly like some new bible written in a language he can't quite translate but maybe someday someone will. He wonders about the alphabet of rainbows. He wonders about words like ecstasy, shame, indifference, penance. He wonders how many buckets it will take until he can shed his memory.

He winds his way back downtown through streets without names cleaning bridges, cafés, mailboxes. He avoids the fountain with the whale sculpture, afraid of the ghostly reflections lurking in the water. What matters after the end of color, he thinks, is to keep moving. Light bends into a hundred colors, but somehow time has only a single arc. The color librarian thinks this is cruel but just.

But Utah has always been a cruel place. The weird orphan of the West nobody invites to the birthday party. Oregon, Arizona, Idaho, California. Saints in the great westward ho. And then poor Utah. A fever dream of madness and manners. Bubbled up like a wart on the butt cleft of nature. A land of addicts relapsing in perpetuity, always itching for the next fix of faith. Afterthoughts in God's retirement. Make no mistake: He is retired. Not out sick, not dead, not MIA, not hold-all-my-calls-during-a-lunch-break. Retired. From the old French. A strategic retreat, a falling away, a withdrawal into seclusion, into the cobwebs of self. Sometimes the color librarian looks up words in the dictionary. Even with most people underground words still mean something up here. Up here, a word after a word is still magic.

————————

He saves the church for last. He cleans the pulpit, the pews, the sacrament trays. One night he found god hiding in the baptismal font, an old man with glazed, red-rimmed eyes. He sat next to the old man and picked the nits from his beard. You can come with us, the god said, you can come home. It's not finished, the color librarian said as if in a trance. He reached into his pocket to share some cheese with the god but when he turned back there was only a rat.

The color librarian stares at the rainbow through the collapsed roof. Tonight, it seems pale, like a bent skeleton of light. It must be lonely up there. The color librarian scratches his beard. It's lonely down here too.

————————

The noise shakes the color librarian from his reverie. It is uncommon but not unfamiliar—the scrape of a manhole cover as it's dragged over the asphalt. The color librarian stands in the church doorway watching them crawl out. A boy. Then a girl.

Toiling away in the library basement, sorting the color into glass jars, he often imagines those hiding in the sewers as dirty, hunchbacked, and blind, crawling out of manholes like radioactive megafauna, speaking in garbled grunts and moans. He can't help but feel a little disappointed they are fair and lithe with childlike faces, taking in the scenery like tourists. They look happy.

Only a few dozen are left, maybe a hundred, the color librarian estimates. The last of the believers, gone to search for a new Eden in the sewers, afraid of this humpty dumpty world with too much color. The color librarian likes to imagine that when they're not coming up here to scavenge they sit in the dark without joy or grief or surprise and sing hymns, recite prayers, play pinochle. He knows she is still there, still carrying with her the memory of all this color.

And the others? The ones who laughed at those going into the ark? The ones who burnt the sky launching bombs hoping it would erase the rainbow? The ones who left in the military convoys? Is it true they escaped into interstellar space? Or did they die in a ditch along the highway, coughing up their insides as the stars blinked at them indifferently?

The boy and girl stand under a dusty lamppost. Their skins are so pale. They're too busy admiring the rainbow to notice the color librarian. They take turns whispering about what they see in the color spectrum. She says a flower. He says a hand reaching down. They are quiet. Then the boy says one of the old gods put the rainbow here as a bridge between this world and the other, and on cold winter nights he meets his lover halfway across the arc and they share an ice cream cone. That's love, the boy says. He leans to kiss her but the girl bends away, folding her arms across her chest. It all depends. What flavor of ice cream is it? she wants to know.

———

The color librarian knows he will never be able to escape color. Years ago, before the rainbow, before his wife, he was in love with a girl. He worked for her father as a bookkeeper. He wanted to marry the girl, but the old man said he must win her love. So, he worshipped her. Wrote her love poems, and listened to her secrets and encouraged her dreams, and never got jealous when she had other lovers, and bankrupted himself buying her cold bright things, but she was cruel and strange and oblivious. Until one day her father told him to forget her, that she was a jellyfish now. Even after he went to the aquarium and watched the jellies happily floating, oblivious, immortal, glowing pink, then purple, then blue, the tentacles of one jelly almost exactly the same as the girl's hair— even then the color librarian thought it was a cruel trick. Sometimes when he looks at the rainbow, the color librarian wonders if this is his punishment for being kind.

The color librarian closes his eyes. When he opens them, the rainbow is still there, but the boy and girl are gone.

The color librarian looks down the manhole into the black. He wonders if the boy and girl will be forgiven for their disobedience. He drags the manhole grate over the hole. He walks to the end of the street, circles back. Uncovers the manhole. He sits cradling the bucket of color, legs dangling into the black. He pours some of the color down there before stopping. It's easier to find your way in all that dark, he thinks.

The air is rancid, his throat burning from the colorless fumes. For reasons he cannot explain, he respects the cruel honesty of this place. Later, he will go down to the basement and pour what's left of the colored dust into jars and try to sleep a few hours before waking up and starting all over again tomorrow. But for now he waits, amazed at the world under this awful miracle of light.

Acknowledgments

My gratitude to Ross Tangedal who rescued this book from oblivion and gave it such a wonderful home. And to the excellent staff at Cornerstone Press for their patience, dedication, and brilliant editorial guidance, with a special thanks to Brett Hill.

To Andrew Rice for his mad, wild artistry.

To John Nieves, Christa Spillson, and Jack Wenke for their friendship and encouragement—I could not ask for better colleagues. To writing friends, mentors, and strangers who helped me revise these stories in infantile form or sent me words of encouragement in the face of rejection: A.A. Balaskovits, LaTanya McQueen, Steve Haynie, Jen Julian, Kate McIntyre, Joe Aguilar, Alissa Nutting, Joan Silber, Michael Martone, and Michael Czyzniejewski. And especially to Aaron Hellem, who once upon a time listened to me wax nostalgic for the desert and assured me my voice was somewhere in all that dust.

To the editors at the various literary journals where these stories first appeared: Kate Bernheimer, Michelle Ross, Scott Garrison, Patricia Colleen Murphy, Leslie Jill Patterson, Susan Yim, Scott Dorsch, Chris Fink, Leah Hampton, Matt Muth, Teague Bohlen, Michael Hurley, Aidan Linder, and Alison Miller—thank you for sharing my work. Special thanks to Bradford Morrow for nudging me to find the proper finish; to Ben Schafer for his revisionist magic; and to Ronald Spatz for his gentle editorial alchemy.

To my brothers, who inspired these stories more than they realize. To my father, who never met a fact he couldn't embellish. To my aunts and grandmothers and great-grandmothers whose voices are buried in here, but most of all to my mother, the saltiest woman I know.

To Claire, Noah, and Violet for letting me spin stories out of the weird things they say. And especially to Audrey, firstborn extraordinaire, for being the social media guru for her old man. And finally—I heard a rumor that behind every brilliant woman is her idiot husband. Thank you, Jenna, for letting me be yours.

———

The stories collected in *Salt Folk* previously appeared in the following publications, sometimes in slightly altered form and varying titles:

"La Petite Mort": *Alaska Quarterly Review*

"A North American Field Guide to Glaciers": *Conjunctions*

"Bookfucker": *Puerto del Sol*

"Of Angels": *Atticus Review*

"The Inheritors": *Pacifica Literary Review*

"Delousing": *Superstition Review*

"The Sprites of Panguitch": *Blue Mesa Review*

"A Whale": *Fairy Tale Review*

"Go Wrong with You": *Arroyo Literary Review*

"The Jump Humping Handbook for Dummies": *Necessary Fiction*

"The Algorithms of Happiness": *Iron Horse Literary Review*

"Forecasts": *Permafrost*

"Every Nerve Singing": *Fugue*

"The Kind of Invisible You Are": *Ninth Letter*

"The Abridged Recipes of St. Marguerite for Fevers, Chills, Visions & Other Marital Ailments": *Los Angeles Review*

"Colorless Green Ideas Sleep Furiously": *Beloit Fiction Journal*

"Rewilding": *Wigleaf*

"Wife No. 57": *Quarterly West*

"After the End of Color": *Copper Nickel*

Ryan Habermeyer is the author of the short story collection, *The Science of Lost Futures* (2018). His prize-winning stories and essays have appeared in *Conjunctions, Alaska Quarterly Review, Copper Nickel, Massachusetts Review,* and elsewhere. He is Associate Professor of Creative Writing & Literature at Salisbury University.

Find him at rhabermeyer.com

BOOK STORE